Playlist

―――

Arctic Monkeys – Baby I'm Yours
Gilmore Girls – There's She Goes
Maneskin – I wanna be your Slave
Taylor Swift – Love Story
Francis Greg – It Will Rain (Bruno Mars cover)
Djo – End of Beginning
DZanum - TeyaDora
Michael Shulte – Falling Apart (sped up)
Taylor Swift – Cruel Summer
Natasha Bedingfield – Unwritten
Joan Jett – Love Hurts
Birdy - Wings
Bruno Mars – Talking to the Moon
Benson Boone – Beautiful Things
Forest Blakk – If you love Her
Tina Turner – The Best
Chlara – Cannon Ball (Damien Rice cover)
Alexander Jean – Sex and Candy
Maneskin - Valentine
Elina – Truth
Seafret – Atlantis
Taylor Swift – champagne problems
Artemas – If u think I'm Pretty
Alice Cooper – I'm Eighteen

I know it's a fairy tale, but no one said it couldn't be real...

Thank you to the hearing impaired community for helping to shape Hartley Knight!

Jared

What does an NHL player do when his dreams are suddenly shattered?
A.) He finds a plan B.
B.) He gets drunk.
C.) He doesn't give up on his dreams and gets back on the ice.

Well, in my situation, none of those things occurred. In my foolishness, I decided it was a brilliant idea to head to a remote part of Alaska, rent a cabin for the entire summer, and nurse my wounds like a cat. Wise decisions have never been my strong suit.

Two months ago, my already damaged knee finally gave out, and I was at a crossroads. I could either take the risk of ruining my body or let go of my NHL life.

I had no idea what to think. I love hockey but hate the media life that comes with it. Okay, I wasn't very famous, but I hated how shallow my life had become. Now, I have a new chance to figure out what I want to do and who I want to be without hockey.

The perfect place to do that is at my grandmother's cabin in the small town of Northwood, Alaska. She moved to Canada two years ago to be near my parents, so her house is now a vacation home. She said didn't know if anyone had rented it for this time of year, so I had the place for three months.

I can smell the salty, cold air as I park the borrowed Jeep in front of the house. I can't wait to light the fireplace and relax on the well-worn leather couch. I might even go fishing in the morning and bake a batch of the brownies my teammates all loved eating when we were on the road.

I grin as my boots hit the ground and my face hits the clean air. Fuck, this is heaven. I grab my bag from the trunk and walk toward the one-story chalet. The chairs are spread out on the porch, and plaid blankets hang as if someone had just rested there. Slightly suspicious, I climb the stairs and take my keys out of my pocket.

The lock sticks a little, but I manage to open it. As I enter the house, I see the vast living room and am surprised that the fire is already burning in the fireplace. It's cold in the cloudy, rainy weather, so I'm glad.

Someone must have prepared it for me, or Grandma must have arranged it. Then, a sweet smell hits my nostrils, and I float into the kitchen like a cartoon character. As the sight of a fruit muffin appears on the large marble counter, I groan loudly.

"Oh, fuck!"

"Meow!"

I search for the voice and look down to my feet, where a white cat looks up at me with huge blue eyes. Grandma's feline friend, Lucretia, tilts her head as if she can't decide if she's ever seen me before while the little collar around her neck twinkles. I thought we had become close friends on my last visit, but I guess she still doesn't like me. That necklace must have cost more than my suit. She's a spoiled brat.

I lean down and stroke her head. Slightly suspicious of me, she presses her face into my palm, and I swear, she furrows her non-existent eyebrows.

"Meow!"

"Hey buddy, you're with me for a while until Granny gets bored of Montreal again."

The cat snorts, pouts seriously, and then turns her back on me like I'm some hapless underling.

She even raises her tail as if to prove her harsh opinion with her ass. I sigh.

I love Grandma. How can anyone be so good to me? Her friend Marie must have dropped off these muffins as a welcome gift.

I grab a large piece of the muffin and shove half of it into my mouth while I pull my cell phone out of my pocket to call my grandmother.

When she picks up, she speaks in a deep, friendly voice.

"Are you there, Jared?"

"Yeah, and this place is still amazing."

"Be careful. Don't throw a big party while you're there."

I only have one friend who lives here and I haven't seen him in a long time, so I doubt it will be a "big party" if I invite him.

My grandmother exhales strangely as I hear the sound of cars honking.

"Did you sneak out on the balcony to smoke again?" I ask nervously. "Granny..."

"Don't say anything! And this stays between us. I won't tell anyone that you smoked marijuana in my yard when you were seventeen."

Jesus, how does she remember?

"Deal."

"Good boy. By the way, thank you for your help with the project I asked you about."

"You're welcome, Granny. Thanks for the muffin, by the way. It's delicious. Marie made it?" I ask, mouth full. The line grew quiet for a moment.

"I don't know anything about muffins, Jared."

Then I hear footsteps, and when I turn around, I see a girl at the kitchen's entrance. She stares at me with her mouth open, staring at me nervously while I continue to eat my muffin.

"Um... hello?" I look at her in surprise, and she tilts her head like a puppy.

"Granny, I'm not alone. I'll have to call you back."

I put the phone down and turn to face the intruder. I quickly look at her tight, frayed jeans, brown boots, and the white turtleneck stretched across her chest. Long honey-brown waves with reddish tones frame her face, and her nose is freckled like the sun has kissed it gently. Her dark chocolate brown eyes still look back at me strangely, and I think this girl is the muffin incarnate. But I need to figure out what she's doing here. Gosh, I hope she's not some fan following me around. I tried to hide where I was going when I left, but maybe someone found out.

"Would you happen to be a Wild Wolves fan?" I ask, she's still looking at me in silence.

She glances at the muffin, and then back at me, looking at me like she has just been hit. Now, I need help understanding what is going on.

"Hello, are you unable to speak?" I ask again, and she shakes her head as if she doesn't understand.

Shit, tourist! How could I not have thought of that? She must be my neighbor, and she's brought me a present. Maybe she only speaks Dutch or German. They are frequent tourists in this town.

"You don't speak English," I smile, "no problem. Thanks for the muffin, but I'm exhausted. If you describe which house you are staying in, I'll come over and say hello soon," I wink at her. "But right now, I'd like some time alone. I had a long trip and I am exhausted, okay?" Still nothing. "Bye then." I hold up my hand as she furrows her dark eyebrows.

"Okay, I don't have time for this," I sigh and walk away. As my shoulder brushes her arm, a tingle runs through my skin, but I ignore it. I open the front door.

"Thanks for coming. Goodbye."

The girl walks over to me with slightly unsteady steps and crosses her arms. I push her gently out of the door and onto the porch. She looks back at me with big eyes.

"Have a nice day."

Then I close the door in her face. Shit. I feel like a jerk because she seems harmless, but she's getting on my nerves with her lack of words. As I walk back to the kitchen, there's a loud knock, and I open the door. Again, the girl is standing there with a furious look.

"Listen, I know I was rude. I'm sorry, but I'm drained." I sigh, and she points to the kitchen.

I watch in confusion as she pushes me out of the way and walks back into the house. For someone so small, she's pretty damn strong.

Maybe she's just another puck bunny who followed me here? Maybe we've met somewhere before? I have to protect my muffins, so there's only one thing I can do. I need to distract her.

"All right, let's get this over with." I take off my sweater and stand half-naked in front of her in the kitchen. Her eyes burn down my body, and I watch as she looks at me with a confused expression.

"Come on, baby. I'm all yours. Do whatever you want to me."

She shakes her head, tucking her hair behind her ears. She's so innocent and cute. What am I missing? Then, she pulls a pad of paper out of her pocket and begins writing.

I watch, stunned, as she hands me the paper, and I read what she has scribbled. I have to check a few times to ensure I'm seeing right.

I can't hear you.

I look up from the page as understanding washes over me, smiling as she points to her ear. My whole body, maybe even my soul, freezes. Fuck! I kicked a girl out of my house because she wouldn't answer my questions, and really, she didn't understand what I was saying. I'm such an idiot. Pain stabs me in the chest for my behavior, and when I look into those brown eyes, my heart starts pounding...

Hartley

I always knew that hockey players were pompous asses, but now I have the proof.

First, there's this big, muscular guy. Who is very-very hot. The bookworm in me can't help but laugh because on my blog, I always write about how every hockey player in books looks like him, and here he is with his dark wavy hair, blue-green eyes, and gorgeous sharp features. He has a scar next to his eye, and his nose looks like it's been broken before, but still, he looks like a nice guy. But I have to remind myself that he broke into the cabin I rented for the weekend, ate my muffin, kicked me out of the house, and now he's half-naked. I'm starting to think this guy is completely crazy, but the look of remorse he's giving me now almost makes me want to laugh. I've often been mistaken for not being very smart and not speaking when spoken to, but the truth is I haven't heard a word since the accident two years ago.

My dad used to tell me I was a hero because I adjusted to the new situation so quickly, but I miss hearing the birds and the water on the lake, the crackle of the fire in the fireplace, or the sound of this asshole in my house. I wonder how deep and rough his voice is.

I clear my throat. I can hardly speak. I rarely get sick, but Jenna, my best friend, gave me the flu last week. I still barely have a voice.

The grumpy hockey player pulls his sweater back on and sits on one of the chairs by the bar with a feeble movement. I watch as he taps his lip and pulls out my notepad and pen.

J: *I'm so sorry! I was terrible to you. Do you speak, you are not speaking.*

I smile and pen my reply.

H: *I am getting over being sick and don't have much of a voice, but I speak. I need a little more rest, and I'll be fine. Otherwise, I'm not upset with you. I'm used to it.*

As you read this, pain will flit across your face, and you will feel guilty. I don't want you to feel sorry for me, but I'm glad you feel a little shitty about your grumpy attitude.
He takes the pad back from me to continue our conversation.

J: *My name is Jared, and I'm sorry. Let me know if someone is ever being an asshole to you. I'll take care of them for you.*

H: *Thanks, but I don't like violence.*

J: *Then maybe you won't like me. I'm an athlete, or I was.*

H: *I know who you are.*

He looks at me in surprise, and then a broad smile spreads across his face as he watches me write.

H: *And I don't like you.*

His face contorts, and his nostrils flare as he sucks in the air. I stifle a grin.

J: *That hurt, but I had it coming. What's your name?*

H: *Hartley*

I watch his lips slowly form my name, his eyes almost glistening as he looks at me.
I stand up and grab two plates from the cupboard. I place a raspberry muffin on mine and one on Jared's plate. The coffee has just finished brewing, so I pour each of us a cup. I look at him

questioningly as I point to the milk and sugar, and he nods toward the milk. I pour a little into each cup and stir with a small spoon.

When I sit back on the counter and push the muffin and fresh coffee in front of him, another message awaits me.

J: *Grandma didn't mention anyone else renting the house. Do you live here?*

H: *The house next door is mine for the summer, but I arrived yesterday, and since they have yet to move out, your grandmother offered to let me stay here for the weekend.*

A grin spreads across Jared's face, and I swallow hard.

J: *Looks like we'll share the house this weekend, roomie.*

Jared

I toss and turn in my bed all night, knowing Hartley is sleeping in the next room. At least she has no problem getting some rest, unlike me. I still feel a little shitty about the way I behaved with her, but I decided I would try to make amends in the morning.

The weeds at the house next door are getting pretty big, so I'll take care of that for her next week and help around the house. I need to try and find my grandmother's hot chocolate recipe and make some for her as a sign of reconciliation, everyone loves hot chocolate.

Shit, she can't hear me. I'd never experienced a girl like her before. She's so sweet and seems so innocent. I got used to women wanting to jump into my bed without question during my NHL career. I wasn't the biggest playboy on the team, even though the media tried to portray it that way.

I dated Meghan for two years. We broke up a year ago when she slept with another guy... I never cheated on her; the problem was that she didn't believe it. Those pictures and rumors spread by the social media ruined our relationship.

With this fresh start, I will be able to have a healthy relationship with a woman who isn't interested in glitz and glamor and doesn't want to be in the spotlight all the time. Someone I can hide from the media with. I won't put my relationship on stage like a theater production again.

I finally managed to get a few hours of sleep, and when I woke up in the morning, a sweet smell crept into my nose. Like yesterday, I walk dazed into the kitchen and found Hartley pulling a batch of cookies out of the oven.

Butter cookies... Holy cow! I don't want to sneak up behind her, so I sit on the counter and wait for her to notice me.

When she turns around, she jumps a little. I *tried* not to scare her, but it didn't work.

She scoops the cookies into a bowl and sets them on the table. Lucretia is perched on one of the chairs, her head raised in satisfaction as she watches the girl busily working around her. As soon as she sees me, she wrinkles her nose and glides past me like I am not even there.

"Good morning," she says softly, and I am so startled by her soft and gentle voice that it makes me jump. Maybe it's just the knowledge that I haven't heard her speak before, but I like hearing it.

"Good morning," I replied, then remembered the notepad. I reach for it, but Hartley stops me.

"If you speak clearly, I'll understand what you're saying."

"What have you baked? It smells like Butter cookies?" I try to ask clearly, and she laughs softly. That sound...

"You don't have to speak so dramatically, Jared."

She said my name, and I realize I'd like to hear say it again.

"You guessed right, I made Butter cookies and honey butter," she says as she pushes the jar over to me.

I groan audibly as I take the hot cookie. When I bite into it, it's like an instant orgasm. My mouth burns, but I don't care.

"You athletes must eat a lot."

She signs as she continues to talk, and I must make a questionable facial expression as I watch her.

"Sorry, I always sign while I'm talking," she signs again. "My doctor says I shouldn't stop talking if I plan to go through with the surgery. I don't want to start at a disadvantage. But sometimes it's exhausting to speak, so let me know if you don't understand what I'm trying to say".

"Was it hard to learn sign language?" I ask, but she doesn't answer right away. She shakes her head as if she doesn't understand, so I repeat more slowly.

"Oh, it's not that hard; you get used to it quickly."

"So, can your hearing ever be fixed?" I point to my ear. "I hope that didn't come off as offensive. I'm genuinely interested in understanding what you're going through."

"Yes, my hearing could potentially be restored with surgery, but I haven't had one yet. I don't have the money to travel to another doctor, and the waiting list here is months long," she shrugs. "And truthfully, I'm scared. I'm pretty used to signing and the silence.

It must make her nervous to think about hearing voices and sounds again, but I can see the excitement in her eyes. I feel an inexplicable urge to help her, even though I barely know her.

"I really... like your voice," I confess.

Hartley grins.

"What happened? If you don't mind me asking?"

She sighs heavily as she pours coffee into two cups.

"Car accident. Two years ago, I was driving home in a snowstorm. The roads were slippery and I could barely see anything around me. I lost control of the car and slid off the road. My car ran into the side rail and I hit my head; it caused damage to my eardrums."

"Shit, I'm sorry," I say. "Are you okay now? Can you hear anything at all?"

"Nope. But there is a sensation of sound, if that makes any sense. The easiest way to describe it is like there is a hum in my ears, but I don't actually hear it. Sometimes, it's hard to remember what sounds were like before I lost my hearing. I've had people not wanting to date me because of it, but I hope one day I'll meet someone who won't have a problem with it."

I want to stand up and beat my chest and tell her that I would love to go out with her, but I don't want to scare her away so quickly.

"I heard about your injury."

"So, you like hockey?"

"I've only watched a few games. I am not big on sports. But, I have to be honest, The Wild Wolves are not my favorite team."

"I'll change your mind," I smile. "Who is your favorite team?"

"The Lion Knights."

I tense up. Of course, that team was one of our biggest rivals.

15

"Honey, you have terrible taste," I shake my head, which makes her laugh again. At that moment, I decided I love the sound of her laugh and would like to listen to it all day.

Hartley clears her throat.

"Let's just continue to write instead! It's a little easier for me while my voice still heals."

I nod and pull the notepad towards me.

When she smiles, two deep dimples appear on her cheeks, and I want so badly to just reach my hands up to her face and feel them beneath my fingers, but I remind myself that, after yesterday, I don't want to give her any more reasons to think that I'm insane.

H: *When was the last time you were here?*

J: *Two years ago, when Grandma still lived here.*

H: *So you know the area pretty well, then. Have you ever been to one of the Sunday morning markets?*

J: *It's been a long time since I've been to one. I want to go again.*

H: *I'd like to buy some fresh fruit. If you want, we can go together.*

I see a slight blush streak across her face and suppress a grin. It's been a long time since a girl was embarrassed by me. Usually, they took the initiative because they wanted to fuck me shamelessly. It's a nice change.

J: *If it's for another delicious baked treat, I'd go to the ends of the earth with you.*

"Hello!" a familiar voice calls from the living room, and then I hear the door slam shut. We both get up from the counter as my friend Danny walks into the kitchen. Suddenly, he stops, his eyes fixed on the girl behind me. A wide smile spreads across her face.

"Well, that was fast. How long has it been since I've seen you with a woman? Maybe a year?" Danny questions.

"Hey man, very funny," I say sarcastically.

Danny's eyes narrow to slits when he leans his head to see who is behind me clearer. A shadow of recognition falls across his face.

"Hartley?"

Hartley steps out from beside me and waves to Danny. I had no idea they knew each other.

Danny looks stunned as she heads for the door.

"I'll check on the neighbors, see if they've moved out," she says quietly, quickly evading my best friend's questioning gaze.

I continue to watch her every move when I suddenly feel Danny's stern scowl staring directly at me.

"No!" He states blatantly, with a hint of a growl in his tone.

"What?" I ask back with as much innocence as I can muster.

"Not her!" he announces. "That girl is the heart and soul of this town! You can't fuck her!"

"I wasn't going to fuck her!"

Okay, I was secretly hoping that I would get a chance to, but I'm not saying it out loud.

"She was simply staying here temporarily while she waited for the current tenants next door to move out. I am not trying to get with her or anything. Nothing happened. Besides, you know me, I haven't had a one-night stand in a long time, you asshole."

"Yeah, but the whole Meghan scandal and the NHL rumors. Don't drag her into this. She's... fragile."

"She's the farthest thing from 'fragile!'" I say this because I can see her strength vividly in the short time I have known her. "I'm not here to have sex with a girl and then ghost her. Why doesn't anyone date her anyway?"

"It's not easy to get a girl like her," he smiles. "Shit, man, you were supposed to let me know when you got into town." He gives me a bear hug that almost breaks my bones, but I return the favor. I haven't seen this asshole in a long time. "Maggie is pestering me about when she can see you." Maggie is Danny's girlfriend, and they are the closest to me here.

"Ah, what does she think about your new look?"

His brown hair is now cropped on both sides, and he seems to have put on more muscle.

"By the way, sorry about not calling you yesterday, but I was surprised to find a girl here who doesn't understand what I'm saying. Fuck, I thought she wanted something from me... I'm such a dick," I push hard into my hair as my friend laughs out loud.

"I'm not mad, bro. Listen, tomorrow I have to work on the boat to help my grandpa, but we can grab a beer tonight."

"I'm in. I'm going to the market with Hartley anyways."

Danny grins.

"Not to burst your bubble, but," he leans close, "Hartley's dad is the police commissioner."

Well, that's fucking great.

Hartley

The Belgian couple moved out early this morning, so I'm relieved to be leaving Jared's house as soon as possible.

He seems like a nice guy, but I don't think it's a good idea for me to live with him. It's been a long time since I've been with a guy, and I miss dating, but with everyone looking at me like a bird with broken wings, it's tough for me to get involved with anyone.

Jared seems like the type of guy that would be fun to hang out with one night, but when I briefly caught a glimpse of his lips and what he was saying to Danny, I drew the line. He doesn't want anything from me, so the thought of anything happening between us is a lost cause. The timing of the neighbor's departure is probably best for the both of us.

I head back to Jared's chalet, where I find him waiting on the porch.

"So, is the house clear?"

I nod.

"Oh... well, okay. I'll help you move your stuff."

I nod again, but he stands there, still staring at me. I shift from one foot to the other in confusion. He's still looking at me. Why is he looking at me? Why has he stopped moving?

Okay, now he takes a step, not towards the house, but towards me, and finally, he freezes as if surprised by what he is doing.

And then he takes a sharp breath, scratches the back of his head, and takes his eyes off me. Well, that was weird. When I walk towards the front door, my hand brushes against his, and I try to push away the vibration that runs through my skin.

I can feel him walking behind me, almost shaking the wooden floor.

Jared finally rushes into my room and grabs my two suitcases with both hands. He rushes past me through the living room and out of the house in a hurry, his behavior could be taken as a bit offensive, but I just laugh.

I watch as he rubs his jaw before entering my house, looks at the weeds in the yard, nods firmly, and disappears into my cabin. A few minutes later, he steps firmly back out onto the porch as I arrive.

"I put your bags in the bigger room." I couldn't quite read his lips, but I think he said something like that.

"Perfect. I appreciate your help."

As if he knows I'm having difficulty, he becomes more articulate and gestures, and I stifle a grin.

"Do you still want to go to the market with me?" He looks at me softly. I nod, and he exhales in relief as if a ton of weight has been lifted from his shoulders.

"Great, I thought you possibly changed your mind."

"Why?"

"Just wanted to make sure you weren't backing out. You don't know me yet, but I want us to be friends. For some reason, I think you'll be a good influence on me."

This makes me think for a moment.

"And you'll be a good influence on me?" I ask.

A gentle smile tugs at his sassy lips.

"I'm very confident that I will most likely not be a good influence on you," he says proudly.

I ask Jared for some time to explore my place and unpack my bags. It's a similar layout to Jared's, but my fireplace is much smaller, though the kitchen is similarly walled off from the living room. It's cleaner, and the windows are slightly oversized, letting more light into the room. I don't have two giant chairs beside the sofa to curl up with a book like he does, but it's perfect.

I change out of my jeans and thin sweater because today's sun is almost scorching my skin after last night's downpour. I choose a floral print dress, Jenna always says the green shade of the dress brings out my eyes and freckles, which I've grown quite fond of over the years. It also has a subtle but sexy cutout on the thigh, and the neckline gives my breasts a lovely shape. I am definitely not thinking about what Jared will think when he sees me in this dress.

I grab my bag for the market, and as I walk out the door, Jared turns to me as I walk towards the Jeep. His eyes graze over me, then his elbow slips on the hood, and he falls.

"Jesus!"

I run off the porch straight towards him.

"Are you okay?" I ask worriedly, and he quickly straightens up and ruffles his hair.

"Yes, YES!" He looks like he's going to scream. "You... look wonderful."

His look of adoration sends a blush down my cheeks to my neck. I remember what I saw him say to Danny, so I quickly ignore the feelings.

"Thanks. Are you ready to go?" I nod in the direction of the car, and he opens the door for me—a real gentleman.

While I wait for him to get in, I adjust the skirt on my thighs and let out a big sigh.

The tension in the car is still palpable when we start, but it soon thaws. Jared wanted to turn on the radio but then changed his mind. Despite my assurances that it wouldn't bother me, he didn't want to, so we settled into a deep and calm silence unlike anything I've experienced in the past two years.

The sun shines warmly through the rolled-down window, warming my senses as we drive down the road surrounded by giant pines.

I shouldn't be afraid of the procedure. Everything has its risks, but it will all be worth it if I can regain my hearing. Music and the sounds of nature would become part of my everyday life again, even if it would be overwhelming at first.

I try to give directions to Jared as we enter the market parking lot. It's cute how he tries to speak clearly so I can read his lips.

"Is everything okay? You were acting a little distant in the car."

"I was thinking about the operation and my fears."

"Let's get out and talk about it."

I jump out of the car and take a deep breath. The smell of baked goods, fruits, and vegetables wafts through the air, enveloping my sense of smell. I'm planning to make a vegetable pesto pasta and a fresh fruit salad today. Since my accident, I've spent a lot of time learning how to cook, researching new recipes, and coming up with various combinations of my favorite dishes. If Jared plays his cards right, I might take something over to him.

"Why are you grinning?"

"Oh, nothing. So, the surgery. It's called a tympanoplasty, where they repair the eardrum. As I said before, there's a very long waiting list." I watch him as we walk to the booths. "A doctor flies in every few months to do the tests and the surgeries. If I am lucky, I might have a chance to get in next year."

"And is there any chance of someone doing it privately? Or being moved up on the waiting list?"

"Yes, but like I said, I don't have the funds," I sigh. "So I'll wait, but I'm good at this. I think I've adjusted pretty well to being unable to hear." I shrug and bite my lip as I enter the first row of stalls. I stop right at the tomato and cabbage stand. "I love my life, but still, I look forward to returning..."

"Back to the way things were?" he asks with concentration.

"I'll never be the same, Jared," I straighten. "And that's okay. I love who I've become."

He gives me a gentle smile.

"Thank you for sharing that with me. By the way, I noticed you aren't wearing hearing aids.

"A lot of people don't. I can't pick up sounds any better, so I don't wear them."

"Grandma had the same problem and hated wearing them; she said they didn't help."

"Okay, now it's your turn. A question for a question." I wink and pick up a tomato to sniff. I ask the older man for a bigger one.

"All right, cheeky girl, ask me anything. What do you want to know?"

He holds out my bag for me to put the fresh tomatoes in, and we move on. Margie, the florist, is already waving from a distance, and I smile at her.

"I heard your injury was pretty bad, so you had to give up the sport."

He casts a tight-lipped smile at me, and I can see the sadness in his eyes.

"I might have done a little research on you," I admit because I didn't get much information on Jared. But the word is out in town. "How are you taking all this?"

"I'll be honest, it wasn't my first injury, and I knew I'd have to retire soon. It wasn't sudden. I came here to get a fresh start."

I have to concentrate when he says more, but I manage to put it all together.

"This is a perfect place to start over."

"Yah, it is."

"But hockey was your life, right?"

"I loved it, and I'm glad I could turn pro, but there were lows. Sometimes, it was hard—not the game, but everything that went with it. I liked to retreat a lot, you know? Whenever I was feeling overwhelmed, I'd come to my grandmother's house."

I pause, gathering the information in my head.

"Sorry. Fuck, I'll try to talk a little slower, okay?"

"I understand you, it's okay. So it was hard. I'm sorry, Jared. I hope you can make a new life here."

"I told my Grandma I would stay at the house for the summer, but I like it here. I always thought I'd move here someday."

Inexplicable happiness floods my body. Finally, we walk on.

"I know your grandmother. She's a very nice woman. I used to pick flowers in the greenhouse she ran.

"She's the best. No wonder you were so close. You look alike."

"Do we?"

"Yes, you're both very cheeky," he grins, and I poke him in the shoulder.

I get fresh spinach, corn, and all kinds of fruit, like strawberries, blueberries, and those lovely apples. I also make a detour for homemade pasta to buy tagliatelle for lunch today.

"Someone likes to cook," Jared says, glancing at my bag. "Is it a hobby or a job?"

"I just like to cook. I have a blog where I write about books and food."

"That's cool! How long have you been doing this?"

"When I couldn't start university on time because of the accident, I wanted to find a passion, and this was it. So I escaped into books and cooking".

"Have you started university since then? "I started two years ago; I'm in my last year. I'm studying design. It's a bit complicated, but luckily, I have a caption device that records what the professors say and puts it into words for me and get extra materials for some of my classes. Jenna and I have a few classes together so she often helps me out if I miss something. She studies fashion design."

"Jenna, she is your best friend, right?" I nod.

"You know, you're inspiring." He pauses, studying me curiously. "You're so strong; here I am, like a lost dog."

"I'm not always determined, and I wasn't always like this. It all demands that I be, but sometimes I don't want to be strong, you know?"

"If you only knew how much I understand..." We stand facing each other for a few long moments, and I'm completely mesmerized by his penetrating gaze as if we're looking right into each other's thoughts and don't need any words. I understand him, and he understands me because we have found something similar somewhere between us.

"I saw you looking at the flowers. Come on, let's look around," he waves his hand, and I follow him, grinning.

Man, as soon as I smell the daisies, it's like a drug.

Jared

I don't think a girl has ever been as happy to receive a fresh bouquet as Hartley clutches it next to me in the car.

I told her to pick whatever she wanted. This is my apology gift to her for yesterday. There were all kinds of flowers. Peonies, lilies of all colors, the most beautiful tulips, and she still stuck with the simple little daisies.

Shit, when did I get to the point where I didn't appreciate something enough just because it was more straightforward than the rest?

She takes a big whiff of the flowers and exhales with a croak.

"Fuck, this smell is a dream."

You are a fucking dream!

Did she swear? Something is appealing about such a delicate, sweet girl cursing.

"I'm glad you like it. I'm sure it will brighten up the kitchen or living room."

I turn to her to make sure she understands what I'm saying, and from her smile, I can tell she managed to put the words together. I have no idea how long it took her to get that good at it, but I wasn't lying when I said it was motivating for me.

I parked in front of my house and helped her get her well-stocked bag. I even got a good-sized fruit and vegetable basket; it looked so good on the way out.

Hartley puts the bag on her shoulder, tilts her head back, and looks up at me.

"Thanks for your help!"

"Thanks for coming with me. So, what are you up to today?"

"I'm going to make lunch, then freshen up my blog a bit, and then I'm going to visit my parents in the afternoon."

"Well, I'll leave you to it then; I have a few things to do," I point towards the house. "See you later."

I watch as she walks to her house and leaves without looking back. I have no idea how long I stand there staring at the weeds, but I make a serious decision.

I go to get dressed, and my phone rings. It's Danny.

"Hey, buddy. I'm sorry, but I can't make it over for a beer today. The delivery guy's here, and I've got a truckload of fish to care for."

"No problem. Can I get a piece of salmon?"

"Sure. I thought you'd be sadder that your farsighted good friend took off for the night."

"I'm busy anyway. I want to clean up the weeds."

"There are no weeds in your garden."

Silence falls on the other side of the line, and I kick off my shoes.

"Oh, no..."

"What do you mean, oh, no?"

"You're going to Hartley's, right?"

"Look, how about you keep your nose out of my business?"

"I don't mean that; I've never seen you interested in a girl like this."

I roll my eyes, but he knows me. Danny's a good guy, and I'm glad he's looking out for me and Hartley. I do not know their relationship, but I'm dying to know more about the girl next door.

"Can you tell me about her? Is she seeing anyone?"

If Hartley is single, I'd love to change that.

"I talked to her mom once, and she mentioned how tough dating is for Hartley. It's too challenging for a lot of guys, and I'm not just talking about the fact that she's deaf. I haven't seen her with anyone in years, and maybe that's why she's withdrawn. Not everyone has the patience to get close to her."

I've never shied away from a challenge, and I'm definitely ready for this one. I set the fresh coffee to brew.

"It will be a tough game if you want something out of it. I don't know if you'd rather be alone right now, or if you'd like to meet a nice girl. Hartley is that kind of girl, but I don't know how open she is to a relationship after all the disappointments. She might be more open to just sex because she's been single for a long time."

Awesome. I haven't been interested in anything serious since Meghan, but now that I've found a girl I like, what if she's only looking for a physical relationship? I don't even want to think about it. I want to fuck her, yes, but I also want to get to know her and go out with her. I want to help her; I want to please her, and fuck; I want to hear her laugh.

"Way to kill my good mood," I sigh.

"No, you misunderstand me. If there's one guy who could hold Hartley in his hands and have a chance, it's you. I'm rooting for you, buddy. She'd be a good influence on you, and you'd be a good influence on her. At first, I wasn't happy with how you looked at Hartley, but now... I don't know. You are a good guy!"

"Thanks, man."

"Listen, I got to go, but I'll call you later tonight, and then I'll come over and have a couple of beers sometime."

"Cool, talk to you later."

When I put the phone on the table and pour myself a cup of coffee, I drink it outside in one of the wicker chairs, enjoying the sunshine. I don't know what's going through my mind, but I'm thinking about how much I wish she could understand me better and have a more fluid conversation. Hartley is your typical 'girl next door' How she doesn't have a line of men just waiting to take her out, I'll never understand. I'm not blind, she's beautiful and smart. But I really want to get to know her better. That's why I need to find a way to communicate with her more effectively.

I look up different courses online and search for about half an hour before finding the right one.

Sign Language Quick Start.
"Our easy-to-follow course will help you quickly and effectively learn to communicate in sign language."

Perfect. I ordered the course and leaned back in my chair, satisfied. Can I learn on my own? Maybe, but I want to get everything right. I take a big sip of coffee and gather my strength for the big job ahead.

Today I'm going to clean up the damn weeds at her house.

Hartley

I mix the bubbling cream, mascarpone sauce, and fresh pesto, sprinkling a few basil leaves on top. It smells divine, and as I lick the end of the wooden spoon to taste my creation, I groan. Damn, if I could do everything else as well as this well-rehearsed cooking routine, I'd feel like Wonder Woman.

I drain the al dente pasta and mix it with the spicy, creamy sauce. My stomach churns, but I set it aside until I make the fruit salad.

I looked down at my phone and saw that Jenna had texted me.

J: *Disney night tonight, remember? I heard about Grandma Candace's grandson and that you went to the market together. I WANT TO HEAR ALL ABOUT IT. P.S. Is it true you spent the night at his house? You're fast, Mama... you little brat.*

This town is worse than a rumor mill.

I reply quickly, but my finger freezes on the screen when I feel a big thud. My eyebrows furrow as I look out the window into the woods. I can't see anything over there, but I can see more as soon as I look around the corner of the house. Jared is half-naked with a shovel, but I have no idea what he's doing. The sight of his body, drenched in sweat and glistening in the sunlight, sends an unwarranted thrill of wanting through my chest.

What the hell?

I trot through the kitchen like an excited goat. Is there such a thing? I open the door and give him a piercing look, hands on my waist.

"What the hell are you doing?"

He suddenly straightens up, and I wish he hadn't. I can almost feel myself covering my mouth, unable to control myself. Sweat is trickling down his muscular, toned body. My God, the sight of those round, broad shoulders and pecs is like lightning across my body, reaching that sensitive spot so quickly that even I'm surprised at myself and my reaction. It's been too long...that can be the only explanation.

No woman could resist such a sight after such a long celibacy.

My eyes travel down his toned abs and over that slight strip of hair under the light blue jeans. I wonder...

"My eyes are up here," he scolds me when I finally look back up to his face. A cheeky smile hides in the corner of his mouth. "I wanted to help. I hope you don't mind," he shrugs casually.

Yeah, well... okay. Good neighbors help each other.

"Thank you," I say, shifting from one foot to the other and blowing a stray strand of hair out of my face. "I just finished lunch." I point behind me like an idiot. "If you're hungry, come in."

"Oh fuck yeah, I'm starving," he groans, adjusting the baseball cap on his head. Did I mention it's on backward? You get it, ladies, right? "I'm going to take a quick shower."

"I'll finish the salad."

I run back into the house and head for the kitchen. I dish everything up and quickly set the table.

I chop up small pieces of peaches, strawberries, and blueberries, topped with feta cheese and a handful of arugula. I'm tossing it when I see Jared out of the corner of my eye.

A hesitant smile appears on his face, and I try to focus on his black t-shirt and the wet hair peeking out from under his baseball cap.

"Jesus Christ, is that pasta?" he rubs his stomach with a pained look. "I've haven't had pasta in forever." He bends over and takes a deep breath. "Fuck, it's pesto. I'm done."

He sits at the table, and I slide into the chair next to his. His knee touches mine, but I pull my foot away. I don't trust myself right now. I'm afraid that at any moment, I will rip my dress and ask him to make me his because I'm so desperate for some relief from whatever it is I am feeling deep in my core.

I have to remind myself that the guy was already an asshole, but helpful and kind, I assume, not only to me but to others, and told his friend that he wanted nothing to do with me.

"That was fantastic, thank you!"
"Do you want some coffee?"
"Hell, yeah! Thank you!"
I've already had two cups of coffee today but can't say no to freshly ground beans.

Jared

Can you have an orgasm from food?

Because I'm confident I can. The creamy pasta melts in my mouth, and I'm afraid I'll end the pleasure too quickly if I suddenly stuff everything into my mouth.

I didn't expect anything in return for weeding, but damn it, I'll do anything around the house any day if it's a lunch like this.

"For just a hobby, you're pretty talented" I say as she sits in front of me again and pours the coffee into the mug.

"I like to try new things," she shrugs. "I bake a lot for my dad. He has diabetes, so I try making as many different kinds of paleo cookies as possible. The muffins were paleo. I made them mainly for him."

"Shit, I just grabbed one thinking one of my grandma's friends had set them out for me. I hope you had some left."

"Don't worry, I hid the rest from you."

"And the butter cookies? Were those paleo, too?"

"No. But I always try to get farm-fresh ingredients, such as butter and milk. I think they make a much better cookie."

"They were amazing."

Even just thinking about those cookies brings back the memory of their delicious taste, making me salivate. My mother was right. The way to a man's heart is through his stomach, and I think Hartley must have worked some similar black magic on me with the muffins because I've been obsessed with them ever since.

"So, you said you like to read a lot of books. What do you read?"

"Oh, I'm a fantasy fan," she grins. "I love anything about fairies and dragons."

"That's awesome. My sister reads a lot, too, and she has a couple of friends who are really into fictional hockey characters. However, those books have absolutely nothing similar to the reality of the sport. I would know; I've lived in that world. I think we have found another thing in common: I also enjoy reading fantasy or even science fiction books."

"I love aliens, and science fiction is a big favorite of mine as well," she points out.

The perfect woman.

"Do you believe in them?"

"I don't know what to believe, but the universe is too big to be alone, right? Of course, it's exciting to think about whether there are other advanced civilizations."

"You don't ever think that one day, some alien race will come and try to conquer Earth as its own?" I ask with a sly grin.

"Did you know there's a locked military facility on the outskirts of town where they supposedly keep saucers?"

"No!"

"I do," she nods. "I'll send you articles about it."

"I wonder if there is any truth or evidence to these stories."

"I think they're dosing us slowly and gradually so that when the big invasion comes, there's no panic," she sighs theatrically, and I laugh. She clears her throat. "Sorry, my voice is tired. I have to head over my parents house soon, but thank you for your help today."

"You're welcome anytime. Do you have any plans for tonight?" I ask casually, crunching my fingers under the counter.

"Jenna's coming over."

I try to keep my face from showing any signs of disappointment. I don't want to get too attached too quickly, and I barely know her.

"See you tomorrow then, sassy," I wink, and she rolls her eyes. I walk out onto the porch with her and watch as she pushes a white bike with a fucking basket on the front. A fucking BASKET! I imagine her riding that bike through the meadow, picking flowers like Little Red Riding Hood.

Then I hear a strange sound—a soft rattle—coming right from my foot.

I look down and see a baby goat next to me. It's pressing its nose against my ankle as if to push me away so that it can continue. The goat's color reminds me of vanilla, with flecks of cocoa in places. Then Hartley squeals quietly.

"Cocoa! What are you doing here?"

So, the goat's name is Cocoa. Could this get any weirder?

"I didn't know Grandma had a goat..."

"Oh, that goat belongs to nobody and everybody."

I must have made a look of confusion because she quips, "it's a stray goat. We don't know where he came from, but he's been on this side of the coast for months. Behind our cabins is a small barn built by a couple of tourists. Cocoa usually stays there, and people from town bring him food," she explains. "They tried to take the poor thing to a farm with the other goats, but he had a panic attack."

"A goat can have a panic attack..."

"He's not like other goats; I think he's more of an antisocial type, you know?" I look at her. "So he hides in here," she points toward the little shed. It's pretty run-down; it probably needs some work before it crumbles. Don't you, my little friend?" She leans down to the animal, which now has its nose pressed into Hartley's palm.

As if having a narcissistic cat was not enough, I also have a baby goat.

Hartley looks towards the battered little shed at the end of the path with a look of pure empathy written across her face. I study her face and the thoughtful way she bites her lip. I wouldn't say I like this face. That look tells me she's planning something.

Finally, she smiles at me.

"Okay, then... I should get going," she climbs onto the seat.

"Have a safe ride, Little Red," I wave.

"What?"

"Nothing."

I watch her ride away and sigh. I look down at the little goat staring at me, then at his little house. Then back to him, and then back to the house, which is about to collapse. He presses his nose against my jeans again to get me out of the way. How can something be so damn cute? I spend part of the afternoon watching the little animal on the porch. He prowls around the house as if surveying the area. I started my first course assignment by trying to get a feel for sign language. It isn't easy, but I know I'll get the hang of it quickly because the thought of doing this for Hartley is enough of a motivation for me.

When my brain is exhausted enough for the day, it's only four o'clock, and I'm bored as hell. I can't wait for my new job to start, which brought me here in the first place. But there's nothing to do now. Hartley has a life of her own, and I'm happy to be a part of it as much as she'll let me, but I can't be hanging around just waiting for her to have time for me. I had to find my way, too, so I quickly called Danny to see if I could help him on the boat. Danny doesn't hesitate to accept the offer and tells me to come by anytime.

*

I head to the boat after getting off the phone with Danny. I also want to buy some fish from him while I am there. The smell of salt water and fish burns my nose when I reach the boat. But I wouldn't trade it for anything; it gives me a sense of nostalgia for spending time out here with Danny when we were younger. Danny's boat is much different than the mega yachts I spent time on with some of the other hockey players. While those felt pretentious and flashy at times, this boat is visibly full of hard work, love, and care for their craft.

After greeting Danny with a fist bump, he sends me in to get suited up in the proper gear so I can help him. I toss him some amazing-looking salmon, which he loads onto a pallet. I've already picked out a portion for myself.

"That's for me," I point and he laughs.
"By the way, Hartley always orders her fish from us."
I clear my throat.
"Did she order today?"
"Yeah."

"Did she pay for it?"

"She usually does after delivery; why don't you take it to her on your way home? She can pay me next time."

"Put it on my account, and I'll drop it off for her."

He grins and shakes his head.

"Whatever you say, boss."

"Shut up," I say firmly to him as I try to hide the heat of a blush growing across my face from him.

"What now? I'm just enjoying watching this love story unfold. I can't wait to be your best man at your wedding."

I hit him over the head with a dirty rag, and he choked on his laughter and the stench of old fish. A feeling of satisfaction fills me.

"How are you and the family?" I ask.

"You know how the old man is, tough and broody as always; I think the business keeps him young." Danny's grandfather goes fishing often, sometimes for days at a time, and he's still going strong. "Janette and Kevin are having a baby."

"Fuck, man, that's great. Congratulations to your sister."

"My parents are thrilled to have grandchild number one finally. The betting is already on whether it's a boy or a girl. What about your brother? Is he still relationship-phobic?"

"He's just living his life. He'll come around."

Harry, Danny's brother, is five years younger than me and has a significant media marketing firm. He's done covers, posters, and other stuff for many bands. But the guy is totally out of control, and whenever we get together, we usually end up wrestling in the mud.

Danny catches a big fish, and I throw it to him.

"Kevin and I have a bet on you and Hartley, by the way," he says with a cocky grin.

"Oh yeah, what kind of bet?"

"Kevin, bet that she falls first; I bet that you do," he shoots me a wink.

"Nothing is going on with me and Hartley." I try to convince him, but secretly, I am trying to convince myself the same thing.

It's so liberating to work under clear skies and relieve some stress while discussing everything from years past with one of my best buddies. The hole hockey left in me is getting smaller and smaller; at this rate, it will heal entirely very soon.

"By the way, I have news for you," he nods at me. "The high school is looking for a new coach for the team. I told them I'd see if you were interested."

"Hell yeah!"

Even though playing hockey professionally isn't in the cards for me anymore, the thought of being able to share my love for the sport with others is something I would love nothing more than to do.

"Well, well, well, look who's here."

I smile at the familiar voice, and when I turn around, I'm met with Maggie's friendly face. Her reddish brown hair has been cut, which surprises me completely.

"Your hair is shorter than the last time I saw you; it looks great on you."

I hug her tightly and plant a kiss on her cheek.

"Sometimes you need a change," she shrugs. "Danny told me you got back into town the other day. Come over for dinner sometime, okay?"

"Oh, Jared's been busy lately."

Danny gives me a wink, and his girlfriend looks at me in surprise.

"What are you busy with?"

"Hartley Knight."

I'm going to hit him! Maggie covers her mouth, then closes it, repeating this about three times before a slow, omniscient smile spreads across her face.

"You don't waste any time do you, Jared. Invite her? That's an order."

Great, that's great.

Hartley

I walk along the forest road to the chalets, the smell of poppies wafting around me. I even stop to pick a few for my basket.

"Little Red, as in Red Riding Hood?" Jared's words echo in my head, even though I have no idea what he sounds like.

I've gotten very close to nature in the last few years, and I'm glad. School, Netflix, and vodka on Fridays used to fill my life. There was so much I wasn't paying attention to. It was like the accident took away that old part of me, and I came back wanting to experience life more.

When I arrive at my parent's house, my mom had made baklava. I grab a batch and some of my favorite Turkish tea. I spend a few minutes chatting with my dad before he says goodbye to head out for work this evening, and I head home to meet up with Jenna. I deliberately didn't mention to him that I had a new neighbor. I know him well enough that he would track him down and run a full-scope background check on Jared. The little he could learn about Jared might lead him to the wrong conclusion, which I don't want. He can be overprotective sometimes, but he's the best dad, and I love him for that.

When I get to the house, Jenna is waiting on the porch. Her mouth pulls into a big smile, and when she stands up, she yells. At least, I think she is.

"Hello, hottie!"

"Hello, baby!"

I park the bike and get off.

"Wow, is that your mom's homemade baklava? It's perfect. I brought wine."

Jenna comes from an Italian immigrant family. Her parents own the best winery in the area, and they make special wines with strawberries, apples, and bananas.

We no longer have vodka on Fridays, but a little wine on a Sunday night is the perfect way to spend the evening. And Disney movies, of course.

Jenna puts her arm around me and signs, filling me in on the latest town gossip. "We should check out the hot new bartender at Rosie's." She learned to sign with me and was with me the whole time I was recovering after my accident. She's like a sister to me, and I am forever grateful for her and her unconditional friendship.

"There is someone else who is also cute and hot," I sign back with a slight smirk.

"Who?" She replies excitedly.

I nod toward the house next door, and Jenna's eyes widen with a big smile stretched across her face. Her dark hair frames her face at an angle and contrasts beautifully with her blue eyes, which sparkle mischievously.

"You must tell me all about it, little bitch!"

*

I bring Jenna up to speed on everything that has happened this weekend. She listens with wide eyes as she stuffs the baklava into her mouth relentlessly. She responds with firm nods and never once interrupts me as I vehemently sign to her about Jared.

"I think he likes you," Jenna signs.

"He told Danny he didn't want anything from me, so..."

"Or maybe you misunderstood what he meant. You should keep an open mind and see where this goes."

"I think you're right."

"Anyway, I remember Grandma Candace talking a lot about Jared when we met her. I saw her trying to sell you on her grandson," she grins, and I roll my eyes.

Candace did tell me, on more than one occasion, how much she loves her grandson and what a fantastic man he is, but she didn't share more past that. I doubt she had ulterior motives; I didn't even know Jared was coming here for the summer.

Unless...

"Oh my goodness, could she have deliberately not told him the house was occupied this weekend? Maybe she wanted you to meet him!"

No, that can't be it... Although knowing Grandma Candace, I wouldn't be surprised if that were the truth.

"So, when do you start your internship?" I deflect. Jenna got her dream summer job before her senior year. She'll be interning for a traveling fashion designer who taught a few classes on campus. She'll work in the on-site office and hold down the fort while Abigail travels.

"Next week, and I'm so looking forward to it! Did you have your last exam last week?"

"I'm finally done. I'm taking a week off and returning to work at The Lauren Store. We've been hired for the Moonlight Palace project."

I started this job during the spring semester, which is an office job similar to Jenna's, except instead of fashion, it is for all types of commercial design work that contractors or even other artists would hire. The Moonlight Palace project is an excellent opportunity for me as an intern and for The Lauren Store to make a more prominent name for itself. She's working on building an empire in town, which would significantly increase tourism and even help bring in more income from fishing and various fruit and vegetable gardens.

After I graduate, I'm hoping I am offered a permanent position. Boyle, the CEO of The Lauren Store, has been pleased with my work so far, which is a positive, even if he was a big fucking asshole in the beginning. Since then, our relationship has fortunately improved, and my colleague, Eric, has helped a lot. I am lucky I can't hear anything because Eric and Boyle used to argue relentlessly. Artists are challenging people.

"Let's toast to being responsible young women this summer!" She raises her glass, and we toast.

When I think we won't return to the Jared issue, my best friend proves me wrong.

"And here's to mind-blowing sex with the hot guy next door!"

Jared

I wasn't stalking the girl next door.

I just looked out the window and got stuck there when I watched her say goodbye to her friend on Sunday night. I couldn't help it. There must have been some magic that kept me there because that was the only logical explanation.

For the next few days, I rarely saw Hartley and was surprised to find myself missing her. But that was okay because I was making progress in learning sign language. Danny and Maggie even recommended a local school I could attend in the evenings to help me absorb the material further.

Yesterday, I finished clearing all the weeds from her yard, and this morning, a basket of butter cookies with a thank-you note awaited me on the porch.

I've already eaten half of them, sitting on the porch and staring at the neighbor's house again. Lucretia jumps off to the side and pushes her head down so I can pet her. Sometimes, I feel like this cat is opening up to me, but once she gets what she wants, she takes off on me again. I think she's using me now, but I scratch behind her ear anyway. When I'm done, she yawns and takes off to explore the world.

My thoughts turn back to Hartley. When I woke up this morning, I thought I would ask her to show me around town if she had no other plans, and I'm praying she doesn't.

My feet take me next door with involuntary movement. Just as I am about to knock, my hand stops on the door as I remember she won't be able to hear it, and the door opens automatically. Well, that's not very safe, so I step inside to ensure everything's okay.

I hear noises from the kitchen and almost yell out Hartley's name when I remember it's unnecessary. Hartley's sigh should prove that all is well, but I go into the kitchen anyway, only to freeze completely. Wrapped in a towel, she stands next to the counter. Her damp hair cascades down her back in wild waves, and when she suddenly turns, her perfect eyes are wide open, and she screams. A gentleman would turn and apologize, but I stand there frozen, unable to take my eyes off her legs, her glistening cleavage, and her increasingly flushed face. And then I realized she caught me checking her out.

"Fuck, sorry!" I yell, covering my eyes.

"What are you doing here?"

"I just wanted to thank you for the cookies."

I keep my eyes shut tight as I gather what little knowledge I have as I sign my reply to her. When I open my eyes, I see her clutching the towel and giving me a confused look.

"Did you just sign?" She asks. I nod. "It wasn't bad. When did you learn?"

"I started an online course."

I don't mention night school as she watches me with a piercing stare. I'm afraid to move and stand there awkwardly.

"You... you started taking sign language? Why?"

"Because I wanted to make it easier for you to talk to me, to understand me."

She reads my lips mostly because I can only sign the essential words, but my explanation must be enough for her because her eyes quickly soften, and a small smile appears at the corner of her mouth. It's a little cheeky, a little sassy.

"You're so sweet!"

Knowing she appreciates the gesture sends a sense of warmth through me.

"I wanted to ask if you'd like to come to town with me. You could show me more of your favorite places and maybe hang out."

"Jared, stop staring at my boobs."

I didn't even realize my gaze had shifted away from her face. I quickly diverted my eyes back to hers, squinting, before she snorted loudly and walked away from me, shaking her head.

"I'm going to get dressed," she announces with a scoff and walks out. Is that a yes? Not a thinly veiled hint that I'll be kicked out of here. I lean against the counter and wait for her, leaving what happens next to chance. When she appears in the doorway, she's wearing short denim shorts with green flannel unbuttoned down the front. I swallow hard because her half-coiffed hair is still damp, making her waves look wild and untamed.

"Are we going now?" I detect a smothered smile in her voice.

I guess she isn't going to kick me out after all.

"Yes, yes, of course!"

*

I like this little town. It's charming and a place anyone would love to visit.

Even though it's a small, tight-knit community, there's so much life here, and as we meet more and more people, I realize that Danny was right. Everyone here loves Hartley, and I'm slightly jealous that she's so popular. I want some of that kindness, and I want her to smile at me like she did at Mr. Jacobson in the antique bookstore.

His wife, Martha, runs an artisan bakery next door, and as soon as we walk in, all eyes are on us.

Hartley chooses a small corner table for us, and I don't know if it's because she can see I'm a little embarrassed by all the curious looks.

"This is the best place in town for vanilla shakes."

"So you're a vanilla girl."

"I love the simplicity of it, especially the way Martha makes it."

"Okay, but if it's boring, you owe me," I joke mockingly.

Sometimes, I feel like an idiot trying to sign, but I like that Hartley is having fun with me. Maybe I've gone completely crazy.

"By the way, have you noticed how everyone stares at us everywhere we go?"

"Well, I am rarely seen with other guys except Eric."

I tense up for a moment.

"Who's Eric?"

God, I'm glad she can't hear the annoyance in my voice.

"My coworker. Good guy. And... he really likes pretty boys."

I let out a breath I didn't know I was holding.

"Can I ask you a question?"

"Sure."

"You said you were starting a new life but only rented the house for the summer. Are you sure you're going to stay here?"

"I'll see how things go here first."

"And if they don't go the way you are hoping?"

"I have options back home, or I might try to find another position within the NHL."

Walking away entirely from hockey is not something I could handle; I know it hurts me not to be able to play professionally anymore, but the thought of not being a part of the sport at all seems like an awful choice for me. I like the idea of getting reacquainted with my old life here in Alaska, and coaching a kids' hockey team is something I saw myself doing eventually. I didn't mention it to Harley, but I'm meeting with the principal and the old coach next week.

Hartley seems a little disappointed. Maybe she doesn't want me to leave, and perhaps she has grown fond of me in this short time.

"I hope you can find happiness, Jared."

I think my heart stopped for a moment. No one has ever said that before. I know my family wants me to be happy, but no one has ever said it like that.

"Thank you, Hartley. I think I'm close."

And she doesn't need to know that I'm talking about a lot more than work or where I live.

Martha, the middle-aged woman, excitedly brings out the vanilla shake for us, and I'm surprised to find that it's actually amazing. It is so amazing that I gulp it down in a few minutes while Hartley drinks hers slowly and carefully.

Meanwhile, we banter and talk about small things. I find out which Disney movies are her favorites, and I confess that I love Saturday morning cartoons. I'm mentally noting everything she says in case she ever decides to watch movies with me like she did yesterday with Jenna. She tells me that her friend had learned sign language with her; she teaches me a few new signs and corrects a few of the signs I've learned so far. When she compliments me on my speed and skill, I feel a sense of pride and almost stand up to punch the air.

After the shake, Hartley introduces me to her world, telling me about school and her work, how she's written several articles for the local newspaper's arts section as a blogger, and how sometimes she doesn't know what she likes to do, she has so many unique interests.

Hockey and studying architecture have always been part of my life, and now maybe I'm a little lost. When I try to explain it to her, she takes back what she says.

Everything is so honest with her. There are no games or superficialities between her and me in this small town in Alaska, and for maybe the first time in my life, I feel complete despite the many question marks in my head.

In town, I also meet Blake, the shopkeeper, who initially gives me a harsh look, but when she sees how well I treat Hartley, she immediately takes me into her good graces. Then there's Mrs. Waldorf, who runs a strange spiritual shop and tries to convince me to buy some crystals. Hartley is my hero when she pulls me away and saves me from purchasing anything.

Our conversation continues to flow naturally, and we joke about the grumpy old mayor who should have been voted out of office years ago. Oh, speaking of grumpy mayors. Who walks out of a coffee shop with a to-go cup in hand? It's the aforementioned grumpy mayor Bob McRoyal in himself. We avert our gazes and try to sneak past him, but he sees us behind his newspaper. I've had the "pleasure" of meeting him once or twice, and because he hates hockey with all his heart, those conversations never go very well. Besides, he and my grandmother constantly fight at every town meeting, which doesn't help my sympathies either.

"Well, well, well. Jared Zykov and little Hartley Knight," he shouts at us. "I hope you don't intend to cause any trouble this evening?"

"Mr. McRoyal," I nod at him. "What kind of trouble do you mean?"

"Like ordering the hockey players here to burn up the peace among the people."

"I have no intention of doing that, but the road to the cabins could really use some tidying up."

"You sound like your grandmother," he mumbles. "Stop talking and come to the meeting! You come too, Hartley, I haven't forgotten about last time."

"What? What happened?" I turn to her, and she's biting her lip.

"Let's just say I went for a skinny dip and ended up in the tourist zone by mistake."

Jesus!

"Yeah, I had to tell her father about the incident... It wasn't enjoyable, believe me."

"Oh jeez, Bob, anything pleasant for you means you can kick the other guy," Hartley puts her hands on her waist, and I watch in fascination as she comes out of her shell.

"What does that mean?" Bob shouts.

"You're looking for trouble everywhere you go, and everything you come up with in this town is bullshit. A pumpkin festival with no real pumpkins? What about that run when you had the whole town on lockdown and chaos and madness everywhere?"

Is it wrong that I find a flushed, angry Hartley sexy?

"Then you can bring that up at your next meeting, missy!"

"Damn it, Bob, leave the young people alone," an older woman scolds him as she leaves the cafe.

"That was Mrs. Kennington. I love that woman," Hartley leans toward me. "She's almost seventy, but you can always count on her to know all the juicy gossip in town. Oh, and she can't stand Bob."

"I heard that," Bob grumbles, and I pull Hartley away with a quick goodbye.

"Say, do we have to go to this town meeting?" I ask on the way to the car.

"I'm afraid we can't get away with it," she sighs.

"I need to know what that skinny-dipping thing was about."

I can still hear her tinkling laughter as we drive home.

As I park at the house, I almost hit the baby goat. Damn it! I jump out of the car to make sure he's okay. Luckily, he's just out exploring again.

I watch Hartley's face, then think of the little shed again. Well, shit. I should build a fence for the goat, too.

Hartley

When we return to the cabins, Jared kindly walks me up to my door, and I invite him to come inside.

I brew some of my mother's Turkish tea and pour it into a cup for each of us.

I asked Jared to light the fireplace for me since the week of bad weather had arrived.

We sit on the couch and watch the flames while we talk to each other, half-signing, half-lip-reading.

"I didn't live with my parents for long after the accident. I wanted to get back on my feet quickly, so I moved back to my apartment. I used my savings to rent the house for the summer and would look for a new place come fall. The small kitchen space of the cabin didn't allow for much baking and cooking.

"A lot of people could take a lesson from you, Hartley. You're amazingly strong."

I smile as I sip my tea.

"By the way, this tea is damn good. What is it?"

"Turkish tea. My mom is Turkish. Keeps a box full of hundreds of different teas at home," I laugh.

"Wow, Hart, that's cool. My dad is from Russia." I guessed from his name, but it would be hard to deny his features. He looks like an Ivan or a Boris. Does that make sense?

"So she's Turkish. Do you speak the language?"

I shook my head in answer and explained my mom had never taught me, and after I lost my hearing, it would be more challenging to learn.

I feel warm at the notation that he called me 'Hart.'

"Once you meet her, she'll charm you," I lean closer.

"Her daughter already has," he winks at me.

"Tell me about your family. Are you the only hockey player in the family? Do you speak any Russian?"

"I used to speak it, but I am a bit rusty. My grandparents immigrated a long time ago. And actually, nobody in my family likes hockey," he laughs, and I'm overcome with the urge to hear his voice. "My brother is an artist, and he looks just like me. My sister designs and sells children's clothing. My dad and mom are pretty cool. They are both teachers at the local high school. Dad teaches math, and Mom teaches literature, and the kids love them. Of course, they used to come to my games and cheer me on, but I still don't think they understand anything about hockey."

He speaks slowly, paying close attention to me to ensure I understand what he is saying.

"Shit, I've talked too much again," he says to himself. "Did you understand everything I was saying?"

I nod.

"I think I'd get along well with your family."

"When you meet them, they'll probably kick me out and take you in."

When... He said when, not if. That's interesting.

"They always kept me grounded, even when they were away for a while."

His expression becomes closed, and I know it wouldn't be a good idea to bother him with the subject, but he does leave me wondering what he's experienced in his career.

"Hey, give me your number! If we're going to avoid each other for days again, at least I can bother you via text".

We exchange numbers, but in the meantime, I'm still studying him, thinking about his painful past.

49

Text Messages

J: We haven't seen each other for days.

H: Sorry, work has started at my parents' orchard.

J: Are you free next weekend?

H: I'm supposed to go to a bar with Jenna on Saturday night, but I'm free on Sunday.

J: Great! Let's hang out!

H: That sounds perfect! See you then!

*

H: Did you pay for my fish?????

J: Surprise!

H: You do too much for me. How can I thank you?

J: I have a few ideas

H: Jared!!!!

J: Hartley!!!! Just take it. You're welcome. By the way, there's a big storm coming today, so close your windows tight!

Jared

I typically enjoy storms, but I find myself tossing and turning in bed tonight. Hartley hasn't responded to my message since, so she may have fallen asleep.

I'm scrolling through the latest article in my favorite car magazine on my phone when a loud knock on the door has me jumping out of bed.

I pull on a pair of sweatpants and run across the living room. When I open the door, I find Hartley wrapped in a giant sweater on the porch.

"What the hell?" I drag her inside and slam the door shut, rubbing her arm with one hand.

"I'm scared," she signals shakily. "I can't hear you. I can't hear the storm," she points behind her.

Seeing her big, scared eyes boring into my soul breaks my heart.

"Let's get this soaked sweater off," I pull her sweater off and hang it on a chair near the fireplace to dry. I try to ignore her tiny sleep shorts and the fact her shirt is so thin I can see her nipples through it.

Luckily, she was not wet under the sweater, and her hair escaped the rain from the cover of her hood.

She takes off her shoes and digs her toes into the carpet. Her toenails are painted the cutest shade of pink.

"Can I stay here?" she looks at me questioningly. "I'm sorry, it's just... it's scary when I can see the lightning but can't hear anything. It's like being trapped in a box."

"Of course you can stay here!" I tell her, pulling her hand toward the bedroom, not to the guest room where she slept, but to mine. If she's afraid, I want her next to me. Close to me in my bed.

There are no ulterior motives, but I'm glad she thought of me.

"Jared, I..." she says, and I turn to her.

"Get under the covers! I won't do anything, and I will be the perfect gentleman. You're shaking from the cold and clearly shaken up."

She nods slowly, then swallows hard, but finally slips under my thick blanket. I keep my pants on and lie down next to her. I cover us up to our necks and pull her close to me. Hartley's frozen like an ice cube, but having her this close to me is still better than I imagined.

She presses her face into my chest, and I breathe in the strawberry scent of her hair. This is fucking heaven.

Hartley pushes even closer, and I pull my hips back.

I don't want her to feel how turned on I am right now.

I run my fingers through her hair, and she moans softly.

"That feels good," she murmurs, snuggling up to me like a kitten. I laugh softly and slowly run my fingers down her back until she falls asleep. Gently kissing her forehead and hoping not to wake her, I finally close my eyes and let her soft breaths lull me to sleep. It's the most restful sleep I've had in a long time.

I finally know what it means to fall in love at first sight.

I didn't believe in it, until now. I have completely fallen in love with Hartley.

Fuck!

*

I wake up to the smell of strawberries and think someone is in the kitchen again, but no, the soft body against my chest proves that Hartley is still beside me.

I hug her from behind, her bottom pressed against my groin, which is, well... very sensitive to her closeness.

She smells so delicious and feels so good against me. I pretend I'm still asleep when I move my hips back a little, trying not to wake her and also hide the fact I am hard as fuck. I don't expect her to follow my movement and press against me again. Fuck...

I lift my head slightly to look at her, but she's still fast asleep. It could have been an involuntary movement.

I try to fall back asleep, but Hartley presses into me again. I freeze when she doesn't stop; she rubs harder. Jesus Christ, I'm going to hell!

I bury my face in her hair and start to move, too. I rub against her slowly, like a horny teenager, as she continues to reciprocate the movement. Then she clears her throat softly and pulls away slightly, as if embarrassed, but I grab her waist and pull her back to me. No, no, no. She started this, and now she's pulling away?

I feel the heat running down my spine as her butt rubs faster and faster against my cock. I control her movement and nip the line of her neck, and she moans quietly.

"Jared..." she takes my hand, and when she pulls it to her chest, I feel like I'm going to explode.

Yesterday we were friends. I tried to take it slow, not wanting to rush her but secretly hoping we would be something more soon.

I don't know if she's serious or just looking for some relief after a string of failed dates, but I don't care. If that's all she wants from me, I'll give it. If that's all I get, I'll take it.

I stroke her breasts, earning another low moan. Just as I am about to slide my hand under her shirt, there's a loud knock on my door.

"Fuck," I growl, taking a sharp breath.

Hartley looks back over her shoulder, her eyes misty, her cheeks flushed, and I want to kiss her so badly, but there's another knock.

"What's wrong?" she asks softly.

"Someone is knocking on my door," I reply, trailing off and gesturing towards the door. "But I don't want to leave this bed."

She laughs softly, and the unwanted guest knocks again. Fucking hell...

I finally climb out of bed, straighten my pants, and look longingly at Hartley, whose frizzy hair is spread across my pillow. I rub my cheeks vigorously as I run across the living room. When I pull open the door to yell at the unwanted visitor, I find myself face-to-face with Danny and Maggie.

"We brought you breakfast!" they call in unison, pushing around me and into the house.

I don't want Hartley to be found here because I am not ready for them to ask questions or misunderstand what happened last night.

We didn't have sex... We just rubbed up against each other like... *friends.*

I am so lost in my head, and I hope she doesn't think I took advantage of the opportunity.

When I finally pull myself together, I head to the kitchen. Maggie and Danny had already unpacked the fresh bagels, meats, and cheeses they must have picked up early that morning at the produce market Hartley and I visited that first weekend.

"Should I make coffee?" Danny asks as he turns to me.

"Uh...yeah," I scratch the back of my head. I should go back to the room and warn Hartley.

"What's got you in a daze? Why don't you sit down for breakfast?" Maggie looks at me, puzzled, as Danny takes a bite of his well-filled bagel. I'm about to answer when they both stiffen and stare behind me. Danny's mouth falls open, and Maggie spills coffee on the counter instead of the cup, burning her hand.

"Fuck!!!" she quickly moves to the sink and splashes cold water on it.

Danny quickly jumps up to help her, but they stare behind me. I turn to see Hartley enter the kitchen, a little dazed. When she notices the guests, she stops and slowly looks around. Hartley is only wearing a white t-shirt and panties. Biting her lip, she starts to back away and then runs back.

"I don't believe it! You didn't!" Maggie curses.

"Hang on, baby, we don't know what happened yet. What the hell is this, Jared?"

"I can explain," I raise my arm. "There was a storm last night, and she came to my house because she was scared."

"And you were delighted to snuggle up to her half-naked in your bed. Nice!" Danny grins.

I'm ready for an epic retort, but Hartley returns in shorts and yesterday's sweater.

"Hi guys... sorry I almost walked in naked."

"No problem, honey," Maggie laughs. "You have very nice legs."

I don't know what's more intriguing: Hart is apparently on good terms with Maggie, or that Maggie is signing.

"Where did you learn to sign?"

I ask, pulling out the chair next to me for Hartley.

"I had a hearing-impaired co-worker in New York who taught me. Hartley and I have been talking like this since I moved here," she says casually. Then, they continued signing, but I had yet to learn what they discussed. Danny and I watch in a daze as the two girls laugh and point, but I grin when I see Maggie's sassy look and how her following sentence brings that pretty little blush to Hart's face.

"By the way, we wanted to invite you to dinner sometime, but this man here is too busy," she points at me, and I sigh.

Danny winks at me, but I return it with a blank expression.

"How have we never met?" Hartley turns to me. "I know your friends and grandmother; you've been here before."

"Baby, fate has chosen the perfect time for us to meet. We couldn't rush this." I wink at her but wonder how we missed each other. I would have noticed a girl like this a lot sooner.

Then I remember Meghan and cringe. Even though we had a shitty relationship, I would have never cheated on her or paid attention to another woman. But that's in the past, and here I am. Freedom and reality.

Maggie and Danny are talking about what they will do this week and how we could have a night out at the bar sometime. I still need to find out when Hartley is going out with Jenna, but it would be nice for the four of us to go out together. I like the idea of a double date.

They leave after breakfast because they need to get to the boat, and I'm alone again with Hart. I start to clear the plates away to help hide the embarrassment of not knowing what I should say to her next. Should I apologize for breakfast? Why would I? She seemed like she enjoyed it. But maybe she was pretending because she is kind, which makes me want to scream.

"Listen," I turn to her, and she looks at me with a smile. She removed her sweater again, and I noticed her shirt was slightly see-through. It makes it hard to think straight. "Sorry about breakfast. I got carried away with... I got carried away."

"Are you regretting letting me stay here last night?" she asks as she approaches me.

"No, I just..."

"Jared, I don't want you to treat me like a fragile flower," she sighs. "I wanted that this morning. I wanted you this morning, but I haven't felt like this in a long time. Is that so bad?"

"What do you want from me, Hart?"

"I don't know, I just know that I want to live finally, and I want a... I don't know, is it wrong if I want someone to fuck me?" She throws up her hands nervously. "I'm sorry, that sounded wrong."

"I can't, Hart, I'm sorry."

Okay, did I say that? She suddenly freezes and slowly steps back, and I immediately regret it. Damn, on second thought, I really don't think it's a good idea for me to have sex with her. She's not like that, no matter what she says. I couldn't do it because that's not all I want from her. I want more than just a quick fuck.

"How about we take it slow?"

Great, now it sounds like I will slip out and throw her into the friend zone. Why the hell can't I communicate properly with women?

"You don't have to apologize," she picks up her sweater. "It was a mistake, I'm sorry. I didn't mean to ruin our friendship."

"Hart, no..."

"No problem," she forces a smile. "I'll see you around."

She runs away from me like she's being chased.

Damn... why does this woman make it so difficult for me to think straight. I want to go out with her and then slowly tear down her walls. I've never been one to take things slow with a woman, but now I know it's the right decision with Hartley. I want her to trust me, but now I think I screwed up because she thinks I don't want her. I do. I fucking do.

I give her time and try to collect my thoughts before explaining myself to her, but when I go to her house, she doesn't open the door after I try knocking. Her bike isn't there, so I guess she's gone. Which is fine. She probably needs some space, but I don't know when I will have another chance to see her this weekend.

Hartley

Jared thinks I'm angry with him. I know…

But I'm embarrassed, so I try to avoid him for a while. God, what was I thinking? I ruined our friendship by rubbing my butt against his dick in a moment of weakness. You don't do that to a friend, damn it!

I'm sure he doesn't want anything from me, and I wanted to try and convince him that we could satisfy each other's needs. Then he said we "should take it slow." For a moment, I thought maybe he meant going on a date, but then I sobered up when I looked him up on the Internet that night. It was too painful to think a guy like him would want more from a girl like me. The fact that having just sex is out of the question hurts a little, but I can't get over the fact that he's a fantastic friend. At least he was until I started avoiding him.

I'm embarrassed to say that I was obsessed with pictures of him and other women I found during my internet research. Various fundraisers and sports events, and he appeared at each event with a variety of women. They all had one thing in common. It was as if they had all been produced in a Barbie factory. Tall, thin, blonde, and brunette, with perfect bodies and clothes. They all looked like they were living the high life except for one, Meghan. She was photographed in several pictures and was much more natural than the other women. Yet, she shared a similar look with the other girls. She had a beautiful face, highlighted by the most soul-crushing, piercing blue eyes, and it felt like she was judging me from the Google images. So I stopped looking.

I watched some game clips. I had to admit, Jared was damn sexy when he played, and I can't stand sports, but it was… it was a thrill to watch, except for his last accident. I watched it three times, and it broke my heart each time it replayed on my screen.

I couldn't find any more pictures of Meghan and Jared together, and when I did find any of her, she was always alone. Was she a woman who left a deep impression on him? One thing is for sure: I can see the kind of woman he likes now, and I'd like to punch myself in the heart for daring to think I might have had a chance with him, even for one night.

"Are you ready?" signs Jenna in the cafe where we met. I sigh.

"Where's the Hartley you used to be?"

"She was in an accident that changed her life."

Her smile is cheeky, and I love that she talks about my accident freely.

"I was more confident before everything changed!"

"You still are confident, just a little more reserved about it."

"I want to be more open again," I decide.

Make no mistake—I like myself. My mom always said I reminded her of Brooke Shields when she was younger, and if she's right, then why do I always hold back? Who cares if Jared likes a different type of woman? I'm not like them, but that doesn't make me lesser than them.

"If you want, we can have lunch at Carrie's Pancake House."

"I'm afraid not; my brother's coming for lunch today. But tomorrow?"

"I'll hold you to that. I'll take you to the office."

"Thanks, I think Eric is waiting."

*

Boyle has called the team together for a big meeting before work begins on the palace. The architects are already putting the finishing touches on the building, so we are discussing decor and visuals. Eric has already reached the entrance and joins me as I hold the large folder to my chest.

"What's up?" he asks, signing. Since we've been working together, he's started learning sign language, and he's doing pretty well, but sometimes I have to correct him.

"I had a shitty weekend," I admit. "But I'm fine now. I can't wait to get to work."

"Yeah, and have Boyle wipe the floor with us. Do you know about the massive battle that is going on between him and the builders? He's trying to convince them that their work is worthless without ours.

Cool, so we get to play mediator between two leaders again.

We sit in the conference room at our usual spot, and I prepare my notes. Boyle walks into the room, growling. Followed by his assistant, Melinda, who's pacing. She's chewing her lip so hard I'm afraid it will burst. Oh dear, this project can't be going well.

Anastasia is here to oversee the decor, and Sadie and Mark are here to do the designs. My fingers are tingling; I so want to draw with them.

Eric and I usually handle the basics of the panning with several other staff members. Still, sometimes, we're Boyle's designated dogs...

"Jesus, what happened?" asks Anastasia with a sigh. "You started arguing with the foreman again, didn't you?"

"Let's just stick to the fact that we are not on the same page, and we're officially going to war with them."

"Great, another game of working twice as many hours with no paid time off?" Mark thunders. "When are you going to get it through your head, Boyle? It's not wise to do a job twice, decide who's better in the end, and then do it all over again in the heat of the moment!"

A big argument starts between Mark and Boyle. Eric starts taking notes quickly to help me understand what is happening; everyone is talking too fast. Meanwhile, I push my folder onto Mark's desk and nod at him. He starts flipping through it, confused.

"Hartley, you'll be working with the decorators, as always. They need you because they're all stupid bastards!" Boyle articulates ridiculously and unknowingly gestures, a motion that is an obscenity in sign language.

"He told me to fuck off," I lean over to Eric, who just grins.

"No! We need Hartley to draw the plans for us! We're stuck on the east and north wing project," Mark winks at me and looks glumly at Boyle.

"Yeah, I'll decorate," Eric raises his hand.

"Enough," Boyle leans on the table. His fancy scarf falls from his shoulder. "We're not fucking around now!"

"Listen to us for once!" Sadie chews on her pen, almost hypnotizing the boss with her gaze. At least she tries to.

"We are tasked with creating the most fantastic, magnificent palace, and we must do it right!" Suddenly, he presses his palms to his stomach. "I'm going to throw up..."

After a fierce debate, we managed to get Boyle to agree on how we should do it. He reluctantly agreed, and at nine a.m., he called everyone to the Moonlight Palace to meet the project manager, who was spending millions on the project.

When I get home, I can't stop thinking about whether I should talk to Jared or not. I stand in front of my house and look at the half-finished fence and the half-renovated goat shed. I have no idea when he did it, but something inside me is warming up. Did he do it for Cocoa? Because he almost hit the goat the other day, and he's scared? This guy has so many layers to him, and I would really like to peel them all away.

Jared

"What's not going according to plan?" I blurt out as my fingers turn white and grab my phone.

"Mr. Zykov, they are having a tough time in the design department, so it would be nice if we could get some order in there tomorrow."

My first task on the job is to lecture some assholes. That's really great. After that, I'm looking forward to hockey team practice because I don't want to continue to bang my head against the wall 50 times a day.

I went to the high school a few days ago, and they'd hire me even if I didn't know the sport. They didn't have the staff for the job, and it appears the team was underperforming due to the lack of proper coaching.

"We will make it work, I promised my grandmother!"

I hung up the call and saw a car parked next door when I looked out of the window. I pull back the curtain to get a better look at the young man getting out. He runs his fingers through his light brown hair as he adjusts the sunglasses on his head. My stomach clenches. Could Hartley already have found another man?

Of course, she's Hartley. Who wouldn't want to spend time with her? I immediately regret saying no yesterday because now I feel like I've driven her into someone else's arms.

The guy walks through the door. He doesn't even knock! Okay, Hart can't hear him, but let's be formal.

Jesus, I should have said yes, damn it. I'm entirely out of my mind.

I try to calm down for the next hour, but I can't. The guy is still over there, and it's getting on my nerves. I go out on the porch to see if the fresh air will help, but it doesn't help in the slightest.

I hear laughter, and when I look to the side, I see them coming out on the porch. And this asshole... is hugging Hartley. This moment is too intimate for me to watch, but I can't turn away.

I cross to the yard towards her house in rapid strides, and I have no idea what I'm doing. I stop, and when I'm spotted, I yell.

"Hartley! We need to talk!"

Hart covers her mouth and gives me a quizzical look while he snorts and looks at me.

"Who the hell is this, Hart?"

Does he call her Hart? Really? Fuck off, asshole!

"Jared, what's going on?"

I look at the guy and narrow my eyes at him as he stares at me. We have similar builds, making it a more challenging fight if it came down to it. He's the 'guy next door' type, which angers me because I know a guy like that would be a perfect match for Hartley.

"Listen," I pull her to me. "I've thought it over. I'm in."

"What?"

I don't know if she's asking because she doesn't understand what I said or thinks I'm an idiot. It could be both.

"Okay, what's going on?" the stranger asks again.

"Who is this guy?" I ask nervously.

"What?"

"Who is this guy, Hartley? Are you seriously going out with him?"

Hartley is completely stunned, and the guy behind her is laughing out loud. He is leaning against the porch railing with his arms crossed as if enjoying the show. He looks at both of us with a disbelieving shake of his head, then glares back at the angry girl in front of him.

"He's my brother, you asshole!"

I pause and cover my mouth, then close it and repeat a few times.

"Fuck!" I rake my hair.

"Caleb Knight," the guy slowly walks over to me and offers me his hand, which I reluctantly take. "I'm not sure how lucky I am to have an idiot like you as my sister's neighbor," he grins. "I think you two have a lot to talk about. I'll be back."

He kisses his sister's cheek, who is still staring at me. I slowly start backing away to try to escape the volcano that is bound to errupt, but as Caleb gets in the car, Hartley stomps in hard, and I'm scared...

"Stop!" she snaps at me, and I do. "What the hell was that? And what do you mean you're in?"

"I just..." I sigh. "I thought since I said no, you'd pick someone else. I'm sorry."

"Why do you care? You said no," she looks at me doubtfully. "Jared, you're being childish!"

"I know. I know, okay?" I look at her helplessly. "Hart..." I reach up, but my hand stops moving, and I let it fall next to my body. "We need to talk. I think Cocoa and Lucretia miss you. You can't neglect the kids on my account." I say to try to alleviate the tension between us. I'm such a coward, and her incredulous face is just another confirmation. I sigh. "I miss you too," I admit.

A little, just a little, it's as if her face softens.

"Can we forget what happened and stop avoiding each other?" I ask pleadingly. "Let's start over and see where it goes."

"I'm mad at you," she says, crossing her arms across her chest and purses her lips.

"I know what I did was stupid. I'm an idiot."

"Look, I..." she sighs. "I didn't want to ruin our friendship. Forget it."

But why do I feel she's talking about more than that now? I've had so much fun planning how I would finally break out of the friend zone, but what if those plans were completely unnecessary. You can't really predict this kind of thing. Maybe I just need to go with the flow.

"Are we okay?" I ask.

Something flashes across her face, but she finally smiles.

"Yeah, sure. We're friends."

Yeah, she definitely just banished herself to the friend zone because I'm an asshole. I need to fix this.

From now on, I'm going to go into romance mode and conquer this girl like no one has before.

But today, I've done enough. I'll give Hartley time to cool off, then try to win her over again.

Hartley

Eric is still laughing at me after I filled him in on everything that happened between Jared and me this weekend. I assume he's laughing loudly because I notice people turning to us as we walk through the Moonlight Palace entrance. We put on our name tags that Boyle handed out yesterday before storming out of the meeting.

"Sorry, seriously? He thought you were hooking up with your brother?"

"Leave him be; he didn't know Caleb was my brother!"

"No, no. I'm already pissed off that I had to hear it from the town gossip network, not you, that you're sleeping with an ex-NHL player."

"I'm not sleeping with him; we're just friends."

"But you were all over him that morning."

I blush and try to push the memory aside. I thought Jared was hitting on me, but maybe it was just his boner that morning.

Eric got it all out of me early that morning when we went out for coffee.

"I'm curious about the new director."

"Not a director," I point out. "Just some guy with money who owns the Moonlight Palace."

"It's an awe-inspiring place, isn't it?"

It is. Our team started on some fantastic drawings for the wall decor last week. Still, you can't complain about the architects because the layout looks like a real palace.

I know it's going to shine and attract a lot of people to the area.

"I'm glad you finally shared your plans with Mark."

"I wanted to take a chance. I don't want what happened between Brody and I to haunt me."

"He was a jerk."

I dated him before the accident and haven't heard from him since. I heard he moved to Iceland to start a new life. He didn't want to live under the influence of his family anymore and usually took out his problems on me. He never cared about my dreams and was not interested in my drawings or my passion for music. He never supported me, but I gave him my all.

We enter through a massive silver door, so gaudy it reminds me of Boyle, yet it's surprisingly fitting in the design.

Everyone is already gathered in the large room, watching in awe. With its silver wainscoting, carved columns, and sky-high windows, it's like a Disney fairy tale ballroom.

"Wow, did you see the terrace?" Eric points to the windows.

"Quiet, quiet!" comes Boyle's voice from the front of the room. A man in a suit with gray hair stands beside him, clearly already in a bad mood. He must be the foreman.

"We called you here early for an important meeting," the man counters as he looks at Boyle.

"Important individuals are visiting the site today, and we wanted to share some important information with you all."

My God, Boyle. Shut the fuck up!

Our mayor is standing there, licking his chops. He's traded his flannel for a buttercream-colored shirt, and his gray hair is perfectly coiffed. He must really care about the Palace project.

"And the most important thing," he says. "We have to keep up our town's reputation so that not only sports fans come here, but also people who are interested in our tourist area."

I have no idea what he is talking about or insinuating, and I am definitely not looking forward to the next town hall meeting.

Then the door opens, and three men come in. All three men wear white dress shirts, pressed pants, and shoes that probably cost more than I earn in a month. They radiate with wealth.

But that's not what surprises me because I expected them to be very rich investors.

I notice a very familiar figure standing between them.

"Dear colleagues, allow me to introduce our investment manager, thanks to him the dream of the Moonlight Palace can come true. Jared Zykov, a prominent member of the Wild Wolves NHL team."

Eric slowly turns to me, and I burst out laughing hysterically. This can not be happening! In just a few short minutes, my life has become a tragicomedy.

If I thought I couldn't want Jared because I didn't want to risk our friendship, now I have no choice but to bury everything because...

Jared Zykov is going to be my boss for the summer.

Great.

Jared

Well, well, well.

If it isn't Hartley Knight, who just so happens to be on the design team I am supposed to be helping. God, if you exist, you've got one hell of a sense of humor—you really do.

When I walked into that room earlier in the week, I didn't expect to find her there, let alone laughing in my face. I felt a little bad when Boyle reprimanded her.

She once told me about her boss; after meeting him, I could clearly understand what she was talking about.

I was waiting in my car on the beach to pick up another investor who was flying in, Kelly O'Halloran, whose husband is a good friend of my family. I haven't seen either of them in quite some time, not since their dream wedding, but I know they had a love affair that only exists in books. I should ask her for some advice on courtship.

I watch as she's helped down from the battered seaplane, and she makes her way to the car with a dazed, tired face.

"Kelly," I call.

"Ah, Jared. Little Jared."

Did I mention she still thinks I am the sixteen-year-old jerk who once drunkenly urinated on her shoes? We didn't have a great start to our relationship.

"Thank you for taking the job. It means a lot to Grandma," I hug her.

"I've always wanted to travel here," she sighs, fixing her blonde hair. "I look terrible, don't I?"

"Yes," I smile as my stomach flops.

"Rule number one, if a woman asks you a question like that, lie!"

"So that's why you have such a good relationship with Steve," I interject as we jump into the Jeep.

"Steve won't be able to make it for a few more weeks. He can't leave with how upside down everything is at his company, but that's what happens when your husband is one of the biggest stock brokers," she shakes her head.

I will never understand how they have such a smooth relationship. On paper, they couldn't be more different. They work in different fields and are, respectively, in the top tier of both. I'm jealous, but they are clearly doing something right, or there is some magic between them that can't be explained.

"So tell me about this place; what do you think?"

I tell her everything I've seen so far at the Moonlight Palace and think about the work completed.

"What about this design team?" She asks, taking notes on her iPad.

"There was a bit of a rift between them and the architects, but it looks like it's been resolved."

"Great. You're leaving me with fewer messes to clean up, and you have my eternal gratitude," Kelly mumbles.

"There's this girl...," I suddenly blurt out as Kelly drops the iPad and turns her full attention to me.

"Tell me!"

"She's so... sweet and unlike anyone I've ever dated."

"I know the feeling. Before me, Steve only fucked models," she snorts.

"She's so real and genuine, you know?" I look at her. "She's my neighbor, and we're friends, but I think I fucked up."

"If you think you fucked up, I'm sure you did," she nods firmly.

"Thanks..." I tell her the short version of the story until the part where I end up offended because I thought she was dating her brother. "Now I'm stuck in the friend zone again, and being her boss doesn't make it any easier."

"Yeah...you're an asshole! What happened to you, Zykov? Haven't you learned how to communicate with a woman yet? That's the worst thing you can say after a rejection, 'to go slow.'"

"Of course, the poor thing was confused and didn't understand your jealous outburst."

"Fine, but now I'm back to square one. What should I do?"

"You could try buying her flowers or some cute gift and ask her out. But, of course, don't just jump right in. Try to spend more time alone with her. Random touches, looking deep into her eyes, complimenting her. Do things that a boyfriend wouldn't necessarily do," she points out.

I knew that myself, but I needed the reassurance.

"Thanks, Kelly."

"Anytime, Bear Boy."

I groan loudly.

"I'm begging you, please don't call me by my childhood nickname," I say as I park in front of the Moonlight Palace.

As we walk to the entrance, Kelly immediately goes into wolf mode, sniffing around.

Boyle appears in the lobby with a big smile on his face.

"Mrs. O'Halloran," he exclaims and immediately hugs her.

"Who the hell are you?" she pushes him away.

"Jacob Boyle," he clutches his chest angrily.

"Ah, Piper Boyle's scandalous creative director son."

Boyle gives me a fake smile.

"You brought a very charming lady with you, Jared."

Oh, he doesn't know the half of it.

Hartley

Mark and Sadie are my new favorite colleagues.

Working on designs with them in the office is worth every unpaid hour. I finally feel like I'm back to the person I was when I designed one of the wings. I can't think of another time I've been so absorbed in drawing.

"This is going to be cool, Hartley," Mark says from next to me. "I like the columns and the wall sketches. The kids will love it."

"I can't wait to physically get to work," Sadie points out.

"You wouldn't believe how liberating it is not to be followed by Boyle all day," I sigh.

I blow a strand of hair out of my face and adjust the strap of my slouched skirt as I make the final sketches of the curve's pillars. It's been a long time since I've worked on someone else's plans. I'm curious if Jared has done any architectural work or if he is just contributing money to the project.

"I'm going out for coffee. What do you want?"

"A cappuccino," they throw at me simultaneously, and when they look at each other, they clear their throats in confusion. I don't need to know what happens between them or the other assistants who work in the room when I'm away.

I wash the ink smudges from my hands thoroughly and head for the cafeteria. As I walk down the hall, I stop in front of one of the glass offices where Boyle, Jared, and a blonde woman are standing.

I can see that Boyle is very nervous when the blonde woman gestures at him, and I smile. Finally, there is someone who is not scared of him. But my happiness quickly fades as Jared briefly puts his arm around the woman.

Is that the investor he was talking about? Jealousy surges through my body, and I decide to ignore it and move on.

When we first met here at Moonlight, he took me aside. We agreed to keep things strictly professional at work, but everything stays the same at home. I'm worried that this boss/employee relationship might be more poisonous to our newly mended friendship than if we had slept together.

"Hey, girl!"

Eric finds me in the cafeteria.

"Have you seen the new girl?" I ask abruptly.

"Kelly O'Halloran, right?" he rubs his jaw. "Yeah, she's pretty tough. I saw her come in with Jared. You worried, Bug?"

"We're friends, and he's my boss."

"That's not what I asked. I asked if that was what you were worried about. I know you like Jared, and you're trying to hide it. I just want to know that you're okay."

"That's nice of you, but I'm fine," I sigh. "I have to go to the North Wing slowly to drop off my plans and map out the work."

"All right, but if you want to talk, you know where to find me."

Eric looks behind me and points his gaze toward something in the distance. I look back over my shoulder and see Jared entering the cafeteria. His eyes find me immediately, and I turn around quickly. I need to finish my coffee order and get out of there before he tries to talk to me.

I swear I can feel him staring at me; only a few people are separating the distance between us. His smell hits my nose, and I tense my back a little to keep from falling over.

"I like your dress," Jared says, looking over at me.

I am wearing a short floral skirt, showing off my tanned legs, and I have a form-fitting striped shirt underneath. My hair cascades down my back, some of it tousled, so it's a little disheveled, but it looks like I've just come in from the beach after a good swim. I flash Jared a tight-lipped smile and a quick 'thanks.' I allow my eyes to quickly travel down his body. A brief thought of what Jared would look like underneath his perfectly tailored dress shirt and slacks causes me to grimace slightly. The woman at the bar puts the glasses on a tray in front of me, and I take them. When I turn back around, I expect Jared to say something more, but nothing.

He looks right over me and lets me walk past him without even a second glance in my direction.

I guess he is going to be very strict about the boss-employee relationship.

Jared

"That's her, isn't it?" nods Kelly, grinning at the retreating girl.

Man, the most challenging part was pretending not to notice for fear of staring so hard at those perfectly tanned thighs that I'd be rightfully fired for harassing employees.

Besides, I didn't want to interrupt her with Eric.

"Yeah, and keep quiet, please! No one can know I have a crush on an employee, okay?"

"Come on. We fucked on Steve's desk in the office once."

I really didn't want to hear this...

"She is very different from other women you have dated in the past, but not in a bad way," she muses. She seems very nice and sweet. She's the complete opposite of that snake, Meghan."

I don't even dignify the end of her sentence with a response because she's right.

"She's hearing impaired."

"Really? I would have never guessed. She is very confident and bright."

"Yes, she is. She's very strong, and I look up to her a lot. She had an accident a few years ago. There is a surgery that could potentially restore her hearing; she is interested in it, and I want to support her."

Kelly watches with a penetrating gaze; then, her red lips curl into a broad smile.

"Oh, my God. You're in love with her."

"I'm not in love with her!"

"But you are!"

"It's too soon."

"You're an idiot if you think you can decide that. Sorry, Jared, but the girl seems to have no idea of your intentions. If I were you, I'd get in there because you're about to miss your chance.

Kelly's words cause an idea to spark in me. I run to one of Hartley's favorite places to buy her lunch and her favorite vanilla shake before I stop by the design team's office to tell them about Saturday's rehearsal dinner.

When I return, I'm out of breath from running into town to grab Hartley's lunch. Clutching the box, I leave a short note for her to find.

I hurry down the hall and find the auditorium with the door wide open. It smells of paint and glue, but it feels strangely pleasant. When I entered the room, I was expecting something different. Picasso-era paintings or something of the like, but this place is very modern. Various machines are in the room, and people sit at several desks to work on their drawings. It was like walking into an editorial office. There are plans and sketches taped to the boards, and on the enormous wooden table that runs along the edge of the room are sets of paints and pencils. Half-finished and finished models are lined up, each depicting a room or wing in Moonlight. As I looked through them, I realized I liked the designs and the direction of things.

There are seven of them working inside, with Mark and Sadie as the leading designers, who I have the impression are secretly fucking each other. I can always sense those things. Then there's Hartley, sitting at one of the desks, drawing on a tablet.

"Mr. Zykov," Sadie straightens. "We didn't know you were coming."

"That's because I didn't tell you beforehand. We're having a rehearsal ball in the ballroom on Saturday."

"Which means what?" asks Mark.

"You will all be required to attend."

Everyone groans.

"It's like a company ball; think of it that way."

As I approach Hartley, I am met with a puzzled gaze. She's adorned with sleek black-rimmed glasses resting gracefully on her flawless nose, exuding an alluring librarian aura. Instantly, a surge of desire pulses through me, reminding me to regain focus. I quickly shift my focus to her plan, taking a good look at her drawing of the north wing. I understand architecture well, but I've never excelled in creative designs like this. Hartley's vision aligns perfectly with the Moonlight style. The twisted columns and window frames, intricately carved like snowflakes, imbue the smaller wing with a North Pole ambiance. Each wing reflects a curated blend of Northern, Eastern, Southern, and Western cultures, a testament to the brilliance of the design department. Aware of not wanting to linger too long and potentially embarrass Hartley, I nudge the box toward her, prompting a surprised glance before I retreat to let her work.

Later, a message from Hartley leaves me feeling satisfied:

H: *Thanks for lunch, boss. I owe you one!*

Hartley

I still have Jared's note that he left with my lunch, and I get butterflies when I read it.

We agreed to maintain a professional working relationship, but I miss you. Perhaps I've been too grumpy at work lately. So, here's to reconciliation.

P.S. *I adore your skirt! I noticed your frown earlier, which usually means you're hungry.*

Since then, he's been delivering lunch to me daily, and in the process, I've grown quite fond of Kelly. I enjoy witnessing how she instills fear in Boyle, but I can't shake off my discomfort when I notice her laughing with Jared. Is their relationship strictly professional?

We haven't seen each other outside of work in the last week, so I was surprised when he sent me a simple text message.

J: *Come over!*

I squeal to myself in excitement. I waste no time changing into something more comfortable. I'm wearing a plain white t-shirt and oversized gray teddy pants. My hair is in a messy bun, so it's really loose and cozy. For a moment, I think about changing, but I don't. This isn't a date, just a get-together with friends.

I grab some fresh muffins I baked tonight and head to my neighbor's house. I stop halfway and stare in amazement at the finished fence. Jared has exceeded my expectations. Cocoa must be happy to have a lovely new home. The sky is clear, and I can vividly see the stars tonight. The air is a little crisp, the wind gently moving the trees, and the strong smell of pine creeping into my nose. In the distance, the mountains rise like skyscrapers, and I stare at them. I return to reality when Jared opens the door, and suddenly, I'm in his arms. He hugs me tightly, and I'm surprised that his chest is beating so hard. Or is it mine? When he lets go, he begins to sign.

"I missed you!"

He looks over at me, and I see him swallowing hard. I laugh and hand him the muffins, and he looks at them like a child at Christmas. Men and their bellies...

"I see you every day," I point.

"It's not the same," he shakes his head. "You're so close and yet so far. I don't like it," he purses his lips and pulls me into the living room by the hand.

Chinese food, beer, and shakes are spread out on the small table, and two thick blankets are laid on the couch. The T.V. is on—a hockey game?

"Did you invite me over just so you could watch hockey with me?" I ask. "I told you, I am a Lion Knights fan," I roll my eyes sarcastically.

"Yeah, and I thought it would be fun to watch it with you and explain the gameplay from my perspective."

"So you invited me over..."

"For a movie night."

"But this is a sport."

"After the game, we can watch anything you'd like."

"Anything?"

"Anything."

Oh, boy, you have no idea what you're getting yourself into.

*

I'm pretty clueless about hockey rules, but I've nailed the basics—like when the puck's in play and where it should be headed. Jared is so excited to break down the game for me. He even scribbles notes now and then to help me out. I just nod along, pretending to keep up because I'm really just soaking in his passion for the game, and wow, it's a beautiful thing to see.

Meanwhile, Lucretia lounges on my lap, and I stroke her fur while Jared shoots suspicious glances at her like they're secretly communicating.

I nod enthusiastically as Jared shares another tidbit. But he doesn't realize that at this point, I'm mostly in it for the eye candy—the hot hockey players duking it out on the ice.

Jared grins and turns to me.

"You didn't catch any of that, did you?"

"Nope," I admit with a shrug. "I tried my best, but it's all a bit overwhelming for me. I've never really been into sports, but hockey's starting to grow on me, I gotta say."

"Okay, what do you want to watch?"

"How about Mulan?" I suggest.

"You want to watch a Disney movie?" he raises an eyebrow, and I nod. "What about Aladdin instead?" He counters.

"Are you an Aladdin fan?"

"Jasmine's hot!"

"Mulan's hot, too."

"Can't argue with that," he concedes. "Alright, let's meet halfway."

"Belle's hot, too."

"Fair point," he chuckles. "Okay, let's settle for Beauty and the Beast."

Jared starts the movie. I relax a little more on the couch and watch as I munch on a spring roll. I almost laugh at how focused Jared is on Belle's singing. It's strange to see him relaxed like this. He is aloof and grumpy at work, except when he brings me lunch. He usually looks right through me when we are around our coworkers, but then there are moments like this when we're away from work where I can see who he truly is, and it's so sweet.

I must have fallen asleep because I was jolted awake by his hand on the back of my seat near my head. The cat's not on my lap anymore, so I figure she's off hiding again. Jared's scent surrounds me, unmistakable and comforting. He is leans against me as his fingers start to move to the back of my neck, beginning to scratch.

I glance over, but he's still completely absorbed in the movie. What is even happening? Is this what *friends* do?

I almost groan at the sweet massage when his fingers begin to move up and press into my scalp. As he massages into my hair more firmly, lust and excitement rush through my body. I fight the urge to crawl into his lap and ask him to let me ride him.

It's going to be a long night.

Jared

Hartley is like Belle.

That's the conclusion I've come to in the last hour. With her long honey-brown hair, her love of books, and her sweet nature. My childhood dream has come true.

I invited her over to talk to me. I wanted to open up to her and let her in a little deeper. I don't know why I thought she would be open to that because we were working together, and I was scared. So I switched to hockey and had so much fun with Hartley not understanding the rules that I left the deep conversation for another time.

She fell asleep during the Disney movie, and I watched her while stroking her hair. I took Kelly's advice and hope it worked.

As I watch the movie, my mind scrolls through the past few weeks, looking back at how close we've become compared to how our relationship started. I also came to the conclusion that maybe I did fall in love fast. Even if it's just a summer fling, I found a friend a true friend in her. And I want to give her everything, especially the one thing I know she craves.

I want to give her her hearing back.

Even if I didn't know her, I'd still want to do it, because she deserves it.

I don't know what I feel. I've been attracted to her since the first time we met. There's something interesting about her... I feel a strong friendship and attraction between us, and I think... She could be the girl I fall in love with too fast. And I'm fucking scared…

I cover her with a blanket and slide closer to her on the couch. She opens her eyes briefly but quickly snuggles under the blanket and goes back to sleep. She opens her eyes again, and I lean in close and try to coax some information out of her.

"Hey, Hart. What's the name of your blog?"

An incoherent mumble is the only answer I get before she drifts back to a peaceful slumber.

Damn it!

I go into the kitchen and text my trainer to see if she's awake. Almost immediately, my phone rings, and I answer it.

"What's up, Jared?"

"Sorry to bother you."

"I told you you could call me anytime. Did you make a decision about my offer?"

I feel tense at the thought of accepting his offer and moving back home—if 'home' is even what I can call it anymore. I can't possibly think about leaving Hartley right now.

"That's not really why I called."

"Okay then, I'm listening."

"I need your medical contacts."

*

"No, no, no, no. That's not where...," Boyle directs in the ballroom. By mid-morning, we've gathered the group to put the finishing touches on the ballroom, where we'll be inviting a few rehearsal guests and hiring a catering staff.

No matter who tries to engage with me, I find it impossible to focus. I'm on edge from the phone call last night and this morning; waking up to find Hartley gone and the living room spotless only adds to my tension. I shouldn't have gone behind her back; this decision is hers to make. But... if she's given the opportunity, she will have the final say.

Kelly's voice brings me back to reality.

"Boyle, I swear I'll kick your ass if you put those boas up on those poles."

"What would you know? You're just an investor with no sense of style."

Jesus, I don't want to get between them; I instead look at whatever the design team is working on.

Hartley bends down in her shorts, and a bunch of guys stare at her, making me feel jealous, even though I have no right to be. I have no idea how to handle this or why I feel so wrong about something when I am only trying to help.

Because this is much bigger than buying a pretty girl flowers, idiot, this could change her entire life.

"Hey," Hartley straightens. "I'm sorry I took off so early, I couldn't get back to sleep, and I didn't want to wake you."

The two of them cock their heads in our direction when they overhear what she said.

Crap, this is not good; now everyone is going to know the boss is fraternizing with his employee.

"I'm swamped today, Hartley; please don't bother me right now."

I feel as though my own reckless reaction has backfired, especially when I see the venom in her expression. I'd rather be hated than endure the suspicious, disapproving looks that follow me even as I walk away.

I will have to find her later and explain my actions because that's what I do, right? I mess things up, and then work on fixing them.

Hartley

Jared Zykov is being an asshole again.

Ever since I talked to him about last night, he's been all closed off and uptight. It's like he's trying to keep his distance so our coworkers don't get suspicious. He doesn't seem to mind that it could make me look bad, and I can't understand why he's doing it. I should be grateful, but that doesn't mean he has to be such an ass.

I'm going to play the same game; let's see who wins in the end.

"Oh yes, boss, whatever you say, boss, right away, boss," I nod vehemently in a low voice, making Eric laugh. "I'll clean up your mess; sorry, you've got dollars falling out of your ass."

Eric laughs, gasps for air, and slowly, the smile melts off his face.

My whole body freezes, and I slowly turn around. Jared looks back at me, and you can practically see the smoke coming out of his ears from his anger. I notice something else in his eyes. A slight hint of mischief. "Instead of parodying me, you could do that column over there," he points behind me.

I curl my lips into the fakest smile I can produce.

"Yes, boss. This boa okay?" I raise the neon green feathery monstrosity, to which he has already said a firm no twice. The tone of my voice dripped with venom. He may have an architecture degree, but that doesn't give him the right to tell him how to do my job.

"Are you kidding me?"

We stare into each other's eyes, and it's as if he can't decide whether to spank me for my misbehavior or fuck me. Both sound exciting.

Why does this man cause every rational cell in my brain to short-circuit?

"Should I get a fire extinguisher?" Eric quips quietly in my direction.

I hesitate, wondering if I went too far, but without giving me a moment to finish that thought, Jared seizes my hand and pulls me across the room, paying no attention to the curious onlookers.

He pulls me out onto the patio and spins me around in front of him.

"You've been sassing me all morning."

"And you're an asshole!"

"I don't want anyone to think you're fucking me."

"But we're not fucking, we're not doing anything."

"Is that it? Are you still mad at me for not fucking you?"

"You really are an idiot." I cross my arms and stare at him in disbelief.

"I don't want to arouse suspicion. It could get you into trouble."

"Nothing happened, Jared; calm down."

"I can't when you're so fucking sassy!"

"I'm not sassy!" Meanwhile, we're getting even closer.

"Yes, you are!"

"No, I'm not!"

The air between us is thick with tension. We're only inches apart, and the magnetic pull I feel toward him is undeniable. I lick my lips, unable to stop imagining what his kiss would feel like. Just the thought of his lips on mine fills my stomach with butterflies. As he continues to stare directly into my eyes, trying to steady himself, he begins to lean closer. I panic.

I step back, turning on my heel, and quickly run away from whatever was happening between us.

Jared

What. Just. Happened? Did she just run away from me?

"Um... I have to get back to work," she croaked out, before taking off.

There's no way she couldn't sense the growing sexual tension between us. When she licked her lips, I thought I caught a spark of heat in her eyes. It took all my strength not to pull her in and kiss her like a man starved. She just stood there, staring at my lips. Ever since the night of the storm, I haven't been able to stop thinking about the brief moment when I kissed her forehead. As soon as I began to lean in and finally claim her lips, she ran.

I burst into laughter so loud I swear it causes the terrace to shake. With my head thrown back, I run my fingers through my hair and shake my head in disbelief.

Walking back into work after that mind-shattering altercation was no easy feat. When my grandmother first asked me to support this project, I agreed. And as I spoke to the contractor, I got involved in the plans. Somehow, I found myself getting deeply caught up in the process in a way I hadn't since college. It's a bit freeing to step out of the NHL world, even though I'm itching to dive back into hockey, even if it means coaching a struggling high school team.

Kelly catches me in the lobby and measures my face with an all-knowing smile.

"You sneaky devil," she shakes her head, chuckling, but when one of the team leaders, Jason, walks up to us, she immediately straightens her features. "Mr. Zykov, the ballroom decorations will be completed soon. We should let the staff get ready for the evening."

"I've invited several other sponsors to the rehearsal dinner tonight. We need everything to go off without a hitch."

We both nod, fully aware of tonight's significance for the Moonlight Palace. Maintaining appearances is crucial if we're aiming for a flawless grand opening in September. My eyes wander to Hartley, watching her precision as she finishes decorating the arch. The anticipation of what tonight will bring causes my nerves to ignite far more than they ever did before a hockey game.

*

My grandmother calls as I'm tying my tie. I put her on speakerphone so that I could continue getting ready.

"Hi, Granny!"

"Hi, so tonight is the rehearsal ball. Don't mess it up for me."

"Thanks for the pep talk, Granny. You really have a lot of faith in your grandson."

Grandma was a town council member who had been dreaming of this place for ten years but had yet to attract enough investors.

"I'm just striving for perfection."

"Hah, I always knew I was just a money pit for you. You couldn't wait for me to make millions in hockey, could you?"

"You're a cheeky brat," she snorts.

I've always enjoyed chatting with Grandma. She's just so damn cool. A true rocker grandma, with her platinum blonde hair, still dyed to perfection and draped in an '80s leather jacket. Some might find her style a bit over the top, but she's anything but ridiculous; she's a style icon embodying eternal youth. And I can damn well hear her smoking a cigarette in the background.

"Granny, please take care of your health."

I shudder at the thought of losing her. I'm not ready for it, and maybe I never will be, but luckily, the old lady is tough.

Changing the subject, she asks, "How do you like Alaska? Better than Montreal?"

"This place is perfect, but you already know that, that's why you offered the house, right? I'm going to coach the high school hockey team." I declare.

"Um... they're really not that good", Grandma retorts.

"It will definitely be a challenge."

"So you're in it for the long haul?"

"Yes, I won't accept the Wolves trainer's offer. I'll help him from afar, but I don't want to move back. I think I've found the place I want to be," I admit.

"Who is she?" she asks suddenly, and I freeze.

"What?"

"I said, who is she? I know you like the back of my hand."

"I..." stumbling to find the right words. I feel like I'm in an interrogation room. "We're just friends." Except today, I tongue-fucked her mouth, and I want to go out with her.

"Do I know her?"

"Hartley Knight, we're friends." Grandma is suspiciously silent. And you know what's weird? When I moved in, she said she rented the house from you for the weekend, so we had to sleep together!"

"I don't know what you're talking about," she replies coyly.

"Of course, you don't. Did you know we're working on the Moonlight Palace project together?"

"Hm... that's interesting."

"You don't have any ulterior motives, do you?"

"Maybe I did, but look, I was right! You're so sweet the way you talk about her, and the gossip network in town says you two spend a lot of time together."

Not surprising, she's even up to date on the local gossip.

"Grandma, why did you want to set me up with her? And why now?"

I hear her laugh, and I know she's very pleased with herself right now. She knew exactly what she was doing.

"I told you about her a long time ago."

"Really?"

"I tried to show her to you last year, and you blew me off."

"I was with Meghan last year," I sigh. We were on a break, but I still wouldn't have cheated on her. If I have a rule about women, it's this. If we get involved, I don't back out, period. "It was bad timing."

"But not anymore."

I look out the window and see a car parked outside. I texted her earlier asking if she would like a ride to the event, but she said she had one. I'm relieved when I see Eric get out.

"Grandma, I did something..."

"OK, this doesn't sound good."

"It's a good thing; I think I did the right thing, but maybe the person would disagree. I acted without their permission."

"Jesus, what did you do?"

I tell her, wanting reassurance, and fortunately, I get it.

Even though I contemplated it, I never intended to take the decision away from anyone; I merely was presenting an opportunity. Still, I felt the need to hear my grandmother's perspective. Naturally, she manages to spoil it all with a snort in the end.

"You're a hopelessly love-struck idiot!"

Hartley

I put the final touches on my hair before Eric arrived. I created large curls from my waves and styled them as if I were stepping straight out of the 1920s.

My silver dress is a tad low-cut, but it fits me wonderfully, hugging my body in all the right places. With a thigh-high slit, it accentuates my legs perfectly. I opt for a more comfortable pair of heels to match, which, oddly enough, fit my feet like a glove... If I weren't so delicate-legged, I'd definitely wear them more often.

I dabbed more red lipstick on my lips and took a deep breath. I pushed out as much air from my lungs as possible, replaying Jared and I's searing kiss from this morning, secretly hoping it would happen again tonight.

When Eric arrived, I looked at the house next door and saw all the windows were dark. Jared must have already left.

"Wow," Eric exclaims, giving me a once-over as he enters the door. "Jared won't be able to keep his dick in his pants."

I smile up at him and thank him before grabbing my little white bag. I feel like a princess going to a ball in a fairytale castle, except I don't have to leave at midnight.

"You look fantastic, too," I look over at him.

He's wearing a green checkered suit, flared trousers, and patent leather shoes. His hair is combed to the side in an old-school style. I've chosen the perfect partner to take me out for some fun. Even Jenna sent me a bunch of naughty emojis when I sent her a picture of us, reminding me of our drinking date tomorrow, which we've already postponed twice. Eric holds my hand.

"Let's go, baby. We want to be late in style, not asshole style."

*

As we entered the ballroom, my heart pounded. The stage resembles a canopy bed with a white silvery curtain on either side.

Interactive columns are wrapped in various shades of pastel pink and slowly rotate. Soft strands of light stream down from the ceiling through the terrace's massive windows and doors, making the forest and mountain views even more stunning.

Five different-sized chandeliers hang from the ceiling, slowly changing color every five minutes. This is my favorite thing in the room.

I look around and see that all the partygoers are immaculately dressed, drinking champagne, and chatting. Some pleasant music must be playing from the loudspeakers because a few people are tapping this way and that in time.

I search my eyes until I find the person I'm looking for. There's McRoyal and Boyle, and the atmosphere is obviously tense. I see Jason, the site manager, and next to him, stands Jared.

Good God, if I thought the neighbor half-naked in jeans or the flannel-clad asshole was hot, I don't know what word to use for Jared in a suit.

His dark blue jacket is perfectly tailored to his every muscle, pulling tightly on his broad shoulders as he lifts his glass and sips his champagne. He looks around the room as if searching for something. His dark, wavy hair is slicked back, a lock falling forward at his temples.

His slacks are almost too tight against his muscular thighs, and I lick my lips at the memory of our fight on the terrace not so long ago when he almost kissed me...

Kelly walks beside him in a red velour dress, simple but magnificent. Her blonde hair is pulled back in a loose bun at the top of her head, a few tufts framing her face. She grimaces at Jared, then licks her hand and brushes a stray wisp of hair over his head. Jared bristles at her touch; I read his lips as he says, "Are you crazy?" to her.

Ew...

I don't see her response, but at that moment, Jared's piercing green eyes find mine. His tense face relaxes slightly, his lips parting as he tantalizingly slowly looks over me. His adam's apple moves up and down as he swallows hard; I watch his jaw clench. I feel a heat of desire rush through me as if he's going to eat me. Maybe he is, and I think I would like that very much. I swear I can feel his eyes undressing me.

I turn to look at Eric and see Jenna walk into the ballroom in a cute, twenty-something, gold-striped white dress. She spins around but bumps into one of the suits, who scowls at her. I stifle a laugh.

"My God, Jenna, you couldn't be more clumsy," Eric says.

"This is not how I imagined my entrance would be," she says in a sign, then steps up next to me. "You're even more gorgeous in person."

"You too."

"And me?"

Eric's hurt expression is almost sincere.

"You always look good," Jenna winks, and I elbow her in the side.

"Does that mean I don't?"

"Hey, they're giving a speech," Eric points to the stage, and I watch as McRoyal, Boyle, and Jason start to speak as they stand on the stage. Jenna interprets what they are saying to me, but I get the feeling she's not getting across what they're talking about.

"We are assholes; we don't appreciate the work of our wonderful staff. A day off for everyone next week and a pay raise because we are so grateful for all the work done". I'm firmly convinced that Boyle is saying nothing of the sort.

Again, I look over at Jared and Kelly, standing in front of the stage, leaning close together and talking absent-mindedly. I've been feeling tense until now, as if I didn't want to be here, but I've finally thawed out. I still have no idea what's happening between them; they are very relaxed around each other, and they're obviously old friends. It still stings a bit, though, especially after our kiss today. I thought Jared would at least give me a nod or a wave.

When he offered me a ride, mentioning he was already picking up Kelly and I could join them, I declined, even though I hadn't yet figured out who I was going with...

Jenna signs to me, saying we should start dancing and drinking. I'm moving from one foot to the other when I see Jared dancing with Kelly. I want to dance too. Okay, so I can't hear the music, and my sense of rhythm is far from perfect, but I can see what's playing on the giant projector, and there are subtitles, I can feel the vibrations of the melody as it echos through the space. At this point, I am used to being the girl that guys don't ask to dance with. They can't whisper sweet nothings in my ear.

I don't know what comes over me; it's been a long time since I've really let myself go. So I grab a bottle of champagne from the passing waiter and down it. Eric and Jenna watch in amazement.

I'm not the only one surprised that I can still drink.

*

I think I've gotten the hang of this dancing thing.

I laugh with Jenna as she tells me what a dick her boss is, and I tell her about Boyle. Eric watches us in a daze as he sips his fifth champagne, a dreamy smile spreading across his face.

"Lucifer is coming," he says, making horns with his fingers. God, he's drunk as a skunk because he wouldn't dare mess with our boss like that.

He quickly walks away, and I turn around to face Jared.

He nods at my friends and then looks at me questioningly, his eyes softening. As he grabs my hand and pulls, my heart starts to pound.

"What are you doing?" I ask.

"Come on, let's dance."

Okay, it's one thing to daydream, but when the opportunity presents itself, my courage often falters.

"I don't..."

"Come on!"

I let him lead me to the dance floor, glancing at the screen to see that If You Love Her was about to start.

I let out a big sigh as Jared pulled me close, sinking into his touch.

I try to remember the melodies in my head, and it feels damn good to think about how much I loved playing my now dusty guitar, the music I've buried as deep as I could for the past two years. I didn't want to let myself get hurt, and maybe I made a mistake.

Jared slowly swings with me, holding my gaze. His thumb caresses my wrist in a circular motion, making my skin tingle.

"What's going on with you and Kelly?" I ask suddenly, and he grins. I try to read his lips.

"The same Kelly, who's dancing with her husband, who just arrived?" he nods behind me, and I look behind me to see the blonde woman laughing with a man.

"Oh..."

"Jealous, beautiful?" He tilts his head to the side, and I give him a piercing look.

"No!" I lie.

"Kelly's a family friend. I've known her since we were kids, a few years older than me. She's always been like an awkward sister to me." I remember her brushing the stubble from his cheek, and I laugh with my head thrown back. "What?"

"Nothing. So you're friends."

"I told her about you," he admits suddenly, but as if immediately regretting it, he slowly looks at me. "God, you're so beautiful."

"You look great too."

I can feel my head getting numb from the alcohol, but I keep grinning at him, which I can tell he's having trouble interpreting.

"Are you drunk, Hart?"

"A little."

"A lot. Guess I'll have to chaperone you."

"No chaperoning, thank you."

"I didn't ask you. I told you."

"Why do you always have to be such a grumpy ass around here? Why can't you be sweet like at home?" I lean in close. "I like you better when you're not an investor."

"And I always like you," he says, touching his nose to mine. Did I get that right? I don't dare ask him to repeat it, but I want him to say it again.

We look at each other, slightly hypnotized. The tension between us is at an all-time high. Just as I think about walking away, the room suddenly goes dark. Oh no...

I'm standing there, completely blind, and I can't hear anything. Nothing at all. The fuse must have blown, but I can feel movement around me, and I feel like I'm going to be sick. I breathe hard and try to calm down, but I can't.

Then someone grabs me, my breasts pressing against his chest, and I know Jared is holding me because his hand slides to the back of my head and begins to stroke me reassuringly. My breathing starts to even out, and I relax a little, but when I feel his lips touching mine, my eyes involuntarily close, and my body is aroused again, but in the best sense of the word. I press myself a little closer to him. Don't stop...

But he does. I let out a quiet groan in disapproval as he grabs my hand again and pulls me along. I feel the cold air a little later and find myself outside on the terrace under the starry sky, smelling the pines and seeing the mountains.

I plop down on a chair, Jared next to me, placing a bottle of water in front of me, which I have no idea where he got it.

"The fuse has blown. Drink," he explains.

I accept without question and take a big gulp of water.

"Why did you drink so much, Hart?" he asks.

"Did you know Hart is like a heart?" I smile dazedly, and he smiles back.

"You're cute. But now please answer me. What's wrong?"

"Why do you think I drank because there's a problem?"

"Because I can see it in your eyes," he points at me. "Tell me, please."

"I miss the music..."

Something flashes in Jared's eyes.

"More and more, I feel like I really want this surgery, whatever it is. I want it."

"You'll get it!"

"Soon," I smile. "I just wanted to let go like I used to, that's all," I look at him. "And I was jealous." Why the hell did I admit this now?

"I knew it. Hart, what's the name of your blog?"

"It's not very nice of you to try coaxing secrets from a drunk Hartley. Daisy girl."

"I'm not Daisy Girl."

"That's the name of my blog, you idiot."

Jared grins.

"Is that your favorite flower?"

"No, I love poppies."

He shoots me a confused look, and I don't blame him.

"Now you're blushing as red as a poppy," he teases, tapping my nose, which only makes me frown.

"And you, my friend, were quite the charmer there."

"Not relevant." He dismisses.

"Tell me what's on your mind, come on."

Jared leans back on his knees, his blue-green eyes holding my gaze.

"I like a girl. And I think I messed up."

"Irreparably?"

"I don't know. I almost kissed her once. What would you do next?"

Oh, Mother, my heart is pounding.

"My father puts fresh flowers in the vase for my mom every morning. That... would be something I liked, too, like poppies. Maybe she'd like flowers," I stifle a smile and pretend to not be the girl he is talking about. "And small touches. Those are important. Not just a simple hug, but like this," I tuck my hair behind my ear as if someone else was doing it and even sigh. Fortunately, I soon come to my senses. "Now I'm being completely ridiculous, aren't I?"

Something changes in his expression.

"Shit, I'd kiss you right now, but there is still a ball full of people who could see us right there."

It's still dark, but slowly, the lights start to flicker.

"Oh well," I sigh, stretch my head forward, and then... sniffle.

Jared

What the hell is she doing?

Suppressing a laugh, I notice Hartley has closed her eyes, leaning forward expectantly. Shaking my head, I remove my jacket and drape it over her. One of her eyes cracks open, observing me curiously as I rise to my feet.

"While it's adorable you're waiting for me to `kiss you, I don't plan to take advantage of you while you're drunk, Poppy."

She pouts, those sweet lips begging me to kiss them, but then shrugs and leans back in her chair.

I steal another glance at her dress; I swear she's a goddess in that silver wonder.

I approach the terrace doors, and the lights come on. Eric appears before me, hunched over like he is about to lose his dinner. I clutch him to my chest.

"Don't hurt her," he points out past me. "Don't be like this, Brody."

I can't even ask him who the hell Brody is because he pushes me away, stumbling towards the bathroom.

I hear shouting from inside, mostly Boyle's voice.

"Where the hell is the electrician?"

When I return to the balcony with another bottle of water, Hartley is passed out, leaning against the table. I sigh and put the water down. I sit beside her and watch her snooze sweetly for a while before lifting her up and taking her home.

The mystery around who Brody is will keep me up all night; I just know it.

*

Half asleep, Hartley told me where to find the spare key. I nearly scolded her as I pulled it from under the mat. Who the hell puts it there?

I carried her into the bedroom and changed the unconscious girl. I had a hard time looking away from her when I spotted her cream lace underwear, but I considered myself a hero when I put on her shirt and finally tucked her in.

I brought my laptop over and sat on the small sofa, not wanting to leave her alone. Right now, I'm surfing Daisy Girl's blog. The site has book recommendations and recipes that are so neatly organized and it's just like Hart.

"I'm currently reading a fantasy book about a broody, enigmatic fairy king who supposedly falls in love with a girl he's been harassing for years."

Hmm... interesting. So that's what girls like?

Scrolling through the recipe section, my stomach rumbles at the photos and ingredients. There's a picture of the pasta with pesto she made for us the other night.

I'm about to look for leftovers in the fridge when I notice a CD player.

I'm reminded of Hartley's comment today about missing music.

I took a chance and played the CD, curious to know what type of music Hartley enjoyed prior to her accident. As the most beautiful guitar notes filled the room, I was entranced. But when the singer started their rendition of "Cannonball," a realization dawned on me - I knew that voice.

It was Hartley's.

I am completely mesmerized as I listen to the song and wonder why she has chosen to hide this side of herself from me. Perhaps it is too painful for Hart to talk about things that have changed for her since the accident, especially things that once brought her joy.

I tilt my head back as I continue to listen, and I am overcome with anger. Here I was, the NHL star with more money than I ever needed. I splurged left and right. I was invited to lavish, tasteless parties. Constantly surrounded by women who only liked me for my wallet. All the while, there was this girl who might be grumpy and sassy at times, but she was the kind of sweetness that makes your heart beat so fast, and she couldn't afford the damn surgery that would make her life whole again.

Fucking hell!

I pull hard on my hair in frustration. Coming to the conclusion that I don't regret what I did behind her back.

I owe her that much, and that's not all she deserves. She deserves the whole fucking world.

Jared

I hope Hartley got my messages and found the freshly picked flowers with the coffee in the kitchen this morning.

After I locked the door, I put the spare key back in its still questionably logical hiding place. I had an early meeting at the Moonlight to assess yesterday's electrical issue. Then, I needed to stop by the high school to fill out the paperwork for the coaching position.

The old secretary's only comment was that I had no idea what I was getting myself into. I left it at that and took her words to heart. Nonetheless, I plan to assess my team's skills more thoroughly in August.

I texted Hartley during the day to see how she was doing, but she sent back a sleeping cat, so I figured she must be nursing a nasty hangover. I decided to order her a good, greasy meal for lunch; hopefully, that'll help her shake off the last of it.

In the late afternoon, I go to my favorite coffee shop in town to recharge before my sign language class and then for the guys' night out that Danny and I are finally having.

The place is run by a flannel-clad, very creepy guy named Ryker, and when he sees me, he gives me a piercing look, as does everyone else in the room. A lot of people in town are keeping an eye on me these days, whispering about me. I am still trying to figure out if it has to do with my Moonlight investment or my NHL career, but McRoyal has certainly made sure I get a bad rap. Maybe they're afraid I'll bring in the so-called "crazy sports fans."

"I'll take an espresso to go," I order, and Ryker nods.

He keeps his eyes on me as he prepares it.

"You're friends with Hartley Knight, right?"

Well, that answers my earlier question.

"Yes... Sir."

"We're very fond of that girl."

"The whole town loves her," I replied with a friendly smile.

"Then you know that if anything happens to her, you'll have a whole town full of people out to kick your ass."

I tried to maintain my smile but couldn't help the shivers running down my spine. Of course, I had to meet a girl with a town full of mountain men protecting her.

"If that's a veiled threat, I get it," I raise an eyebrow and put the money on the counter as Ryker slides the to-go cup over to me.

He nods and leans forward, getting right in my face.

"And what are your intentions?"

Two old guys turn to me and look at me questioningly. The eyes of the town are literally on me.

"That is really none of your business, sir," I snort. "We're both adults; Hartley is a grown woman with a sense of duty and doesn't need to be treated like a child. In fact, I think she'd prefer us not to be so protective. I know someone in her past hurt her once, but I'm not him. Hartley has become one of my best friends, and I respect her unconditionally. I'm tired of the town looking at me like I'm Lucifer resurrected just because I'm friends with her. I'm not the bad guy here. Have a nice day."

As I storm out of the cafe, I realize I left my coffee on the counter. With an aggravated groan, I tuck my head down, stagger back into the cafe, and pick up the cup. I risk a glance in Ryker's direction, who grins.

"I left this here," I lift the cup and head for the exit. "Sorry, didn't mean to be rude."

I don't need this prick taking care of me before I've really conquered the girl.

"Okay, okay," he laughs out loud. "I get it now. False alarm, guys," he waves down the cafe, and I shake my head and walk out.

This place couldn't be more bizarre.

*

Danny has been one of my best friends since we were kids. He's had my back since I first started coming out to visit my grandmother, but when I glimpsed the group chat with my old team members, a pang of loss hit me. Not because I want to return but because I miss the camaraderie. With many NHL players, going our separate ways is just a part of life; staying connected is always tricky. Some players have aged out, others have pursued different paths, and some have transferred to another team.

My best friend on the team, Cage, constantly nags about what it's like here, how much real estate costs, and what the people are like. That in itself is suspicious, but when he sent me pictures with the contact information of various real estate agents, I realized that maybe he, too, was longing for his old life. Soon, he will have to give up his career and start planning a new future after he retires from hockey. Cage… is a single dad. But he has never spoken about it in the media because he is cautious. I respect that about him.

In a totally unexpected burst of enthusiasm, I texted the group to visit me sometime. Still, I wonder if it's really the lack of friends here, aside from Danny, or the beer that is getting to my head. It can't be the beer; I've been drinking water for a while now to be able to drive, so I guess I just miss these idiots.

Danny licks the foam from his mustache and sighs in satisfaction. He's been working too hard, and it's been a long time since he's been able to relax.

"So I heard you got threatened today in Ryker's cafe. It was to be expected, given the guy she was with previously," letting out a soft chuckle as he asked me.

"Do you know anything about this Brody guy?"

As he tenses up, I realize he won't tell me anything, even though we're friends. Now, I'm even more curious to know what happened with him and Hartley in the past.

"I don't think I'm supposed to talk about that."

"Yeah, when Hartley's ready, she'll talk about it."

Why am I feeling left in the dark? I guess I have never told her about Meghan either. She doesn't owe me any explanations about her history. I've buried it so deep inside me as if it never happened, but I know that I'm just lying to myself.

"How are you and Maggie?" I sip my beer. The fizzy, cold drink rushes down my throat.

"I wanted to talk to you about that."

"God, I hope nothing's wrong."

If there is, I know they'll fix it.

"No, just the opposite, it's... fantastic," he smiles.

"Then what did you want to talk to me about?"

"I want to ask Maggie to marry me."

The glass stops in front of my mouth. I had to process the information; it was so sudden, even though I knew I knew it was coming.

"Fuck, man. That's fantastic," I grin. "Congratulations."

"If she says yes."

"Hell, man. She'll say yes."

"I was going to ask you to come to the jewelry store to help me pick the ring.

"Absolutely. You can count on me."

Too-sweet perfume hits my nose, and I sense someone standing near our table.

"Excuse me," comes a thin voice.

I turn to see a blonde woman and her brunette friend. They're both wearing tops with their breasts almost sticking out as if to say hello. Shit...

Panic rushes through me that they might recognize me, but they don't look at me like that. Instead, they look a little perplexed, but I can see something cunning in their eyes that keeps me going.

"I'm Courtney, and this is my friend Kassi. We're just passing through but are still trying to figure out what to do for the next two days. Do you have anything to recommend?"

"You should definitely check out the fish market," Danny replies with a choked smile, to which the brunette gives him an appreciative look. My friend doesn't notice any of this because he's completely uninterested in other women.

"Fish market," the blonde wrinkles her nose. "Ew."

"Someone's got to eat!" Danny growls as if taking it to heart.

She raises her hands in front of her as if to protect herself.

"No offense, but thanks for the advice. We'd rather skip it." Then she looks at me and licks her lips as she explores my body. "You staying awhile? Can we buy you a drink?" she asks, fluttering her eyelashes.

A massive fucking no, I'm done with women like this, and it's not just because of Hartley. They remind me too much... of the women who used to hang around me in my old life.

"Sorry, girls, it's boys' night."

"Come on," she snorts, leaning back on the table so her breasts are practically in my face. "You wouldn't even accept a drink from us?"

"Sorry, but I'm really not interested."

"You heard what he said, ladies. Sorry, and I have a fiancée," Danny sighs. "I'd rather not drink with strange women if you don't mind."

"So? You're not married yet," the brunette shrugs.

What the fuck?

Shock, confusion...

"Just kidding!" she laughs.

"I think you've got me confused with someone else," Danny exclaims, cracking open his beer. "If you don't mind, my friend and I are going to play pool. Thanks for the company," he mumbles, avoiding the brunette. I do the same. The busty blonde doesn't give in easily and makes sure to press her breasts against me as I dodge her.

Her perfume makes me want to throw up on the table, but I just wave her off and follow Danny.

Thank God they didn't recognize me. It would have been hell.

Hartley

Jenna and I decided to check out her cousin Jason's rum bar this evening. As he's fixing our drinks, I can't help but admire the awesome tattoos on his arm.

Jenna requested non-alcoholic drinks; we both had lingering hangovers from last night's festivities.

"I know just what you need to cure those hangovers," Jason says with a playful tilt of his head.

Recalling our overindulgence from the night before, I remember the sweet gestures I woke up to in the morning, the smell of fresh coffee, and a note on my bed saying that Jared had slept on my couch all night after driving me home to take care of me. When I walked into the kitchen and saw the fresh bouquet of poppies in the vase, I couldn't wipe the grin off my face.

I hope your headache isn't awful today. I haven't forgotten about last night, Poppy. I'll be home late tonight, but I'll knock on your door.

And I'll be waiting, that is, if I can survive this girls night with Jenna that we've been planning for two weeks.

"Great, a sobering drink, then tequila," she grins, and Jason looks at her like her hair is on fire.

"What? Drinking helps with the hangover because when you're drunk, you don't have a hangover. You know?"

"That was the joke of the year, Jenna," I groan.

We get our disgusting green drink and look around for a secluded booth to slip into.

We both take a sip of our drink and then swallow hard with a grimace. This is... awful.

"We're pathetic," she laughs.

Her sentiment has me thinking back to last night. I made such a fool of myself in front of Jared Zykov.

Sinking back into the booth in shame, I remembered I'd made out with him on the terrace. And my God, I told him the name of my blog and continued to embarrass myself by pouting like a child in hopes he would kiss me again.

Jenna was about to say something but stiffened momentarily as she glared behind me.

"What?"

She grabbed my hand.

"Have I told you you're beautiful?" she signed.

"Every day," I look at her blankly, then turn around.

Are you serious?

Jared and Danny are standing by the pool table, but they are not alone. Well, Jared is not alone. A brunette is leaning against the table right next to him with her arms crossed, and a blonde listens to him with interest. Oh wow! They are sooo hot! If I liked girls... They have their backs to me, so I can't read their lips, but that's enough to see what I need to see.

Images of the articles I've found about him and the women he's been with flash through my mind. These two strangers are in the same league as other women he has been with.

I guess I know who Jared likes now and it's obviously not me. I'm struggling with my inner self.

But he kissed me.

That could mean anything. Like maybe, he wanted to shut me up, for example.

He cared for you and brought you poppies, just like you told him to do when you asked him what to do if he liked something.

I wouldn't be the last woman to misunderstand male-female friendship.

I turn back to Jenna, who gives me a painfully regretful look.

"Whatever, I don't care," I smile and take another sip of my drink, but I know she doesn't believe me.

"Let's go somewhere else," she says as she signs, then sips the disgusting drink. I gag at the sight. "Let's go to the pancake house instead."

"I wouldn't fight that idea."

I can only drink half of this shit, but Jenna quickly finishes hers off with a grimace.

"Just don't make me throw up."

We step out of the booth, and I stumble into a hard chest. I look up at Jack Ryder staring at me with a sneer.

"Jack," I nod at him.

"Hartley," he replies with a sneer. He's been playing games with me since my accident, but I have no idea what I ever did to him to warrant his constant torment.

"Let's just get this over with," I sigh. "What kind of bullshit joke are you trying to pull on me now?"

"Me, nothing," he grins, clutching me to his chest. "What kind of person do you think I am? You think I'd make a joke about someone being... deficient?"

"Excuse me?" I say incredulously while pushing away from him as hard as I can.

"Come on. That's pathetic, Hartley. Everyone gives in to your every whim just because you're deaf."

"Listen, Jack," Jenna steps forward. "Come a little closer so I can rip your balls off."

"See? This is what I'm talking about. Little Hartley gets more time for exams. Everyone feels sorry for Little Hartley. You never get over the fact that you're at a disadvantage..."

I can barely follow the movement of his mouth, but the point is made, and even though it hits me in the chest a little, I've learned to deal with this kind of harassment. Fortunately, it doesn't really bother me anymore. "Please, don't spare her. You've probably been holding this in for a long time, and you should probably see a therapist to discuss taking the stress of your little dick out on a girl," Jenna snorts, but I shut her up. I'm interested in hearing Jack's outburst, just in case he finally explains why he's actually mad at me.

His misty eyes peer into mine as he swallows the contents of his beer bottle. Clearly, he's drunk, and that is why he dares to behave like this.

"Baby, your little boy toy is the talk of the town," he says. "Don't get your hopes up. A guy like that wouldn't want anything from a deaf girl. He can't even tell you that he wants to fuck you. Even if he's with you, just because he feels sorry for you..."

And then he stopped. Not because he was finished speaking but because someone was punching him in the face.

"Jesus," I put my hand over my mouth and froze completely.

Jared pushes Jack against the wall and says something to him, he is facing away from me so I can't see what he is saying.

"He tells him to repeat it, motherfucker, and then he tells him not to look at you again or he will fucking beat his ass," Jenna quickly interprets their conversation for me.

Biting my lip, I watch anxiously as chaos breaks out, and just as I'm about to try to get between them, Danny pulls Jared off of Jack. Jason jumps over the counter and throws himself between the two guys.

The blonde and brunette girls scream, and all hell breaks loose.

*

We all got kicked out of the bar.

We're all standing on the side of the road while Jenna and I try to create some distance between the guys. Danny is still growling to himself, and Jared... he's like a restless animal.

The first cab arrives, and suddenly, he's pulling me by the hand behind him, not towards the car, but into the parking lot.

"Hey, hey, hey!" Jenna says, pulling me back. "Sorry, who do you think you are?" she asks Jared, knowing precisely who he is.

"I'm a friend of hers. And you are?"

"Her best friend and I'm driving her home; we were just waiting for a cab."

"I'll drive Hartley home, I have a car. We need to talk," he looks at me tensely like I've done something wrong.

"Then who the hell was waiting for a cab?"

"Me," Jack raises his hand and looks at me regretfully. As he is he about to speak, I cut him off.

"No," I raise my hand. "You said enough Jack."

When I look at Jared, his eyes brim with pride, then beg for my answer.

"Jenna, he's my neighbor; he can just take me home," I sigh.

"I could use a ride, though," Danny volunteers. Jenna hugs me tightly, keeping her eyes on me as Jared pulls up to us in his Jeep.

Ten minutes later, we're zooming back down the dirt road, and the silence is unbearable. I can still feel the lingering adrenaline in the air, and Jared is gripping the wheel so tightly that I'm afraid he will break it. I am just about to say something to break the silence; he speaks first.

"He likes you," he states, with clear disdain in his eyes.

"What? Jack?"

"Yes. I saw the way he looked at you before he came over. He's bullying you because he doesn't know how to hit on you."

"Interesting that you noticed; you obviously were busy having your own fun."

He shoots me a quick glance, our eyes meeting for a moment before he returns his focus to the road ahead.

"What?"

"The girls. You know, I'm not surprised," I sigh. "I looked you up online and saw the kind of women you were with." His fingers go white on the wheel. "They're not like me, and those girls were no different, so I get it all. Sorry I ruined your evening."

"Are you... are you fucking serious?" he snaps his gaze to me.

My eyes widen at his tense body language. I've never seen him so nervous, not even when he kissed me.

He slows down the car and parks quickly.

"Get out!" He says quickly.

I realize we're back at the cabins.

I slowly get out, and by now, Jared is circling the car and facing me.

"Nothing happened, Hartley. Danny and I went out for a boys' night, and those two girls wouldn't leave us alone. I don't know what you saw, but every time they tried, I shook them off. What's all this about me dating women?"

"I was just... you were nice to me, kissed me, and brought me poppies this morning. I thought maybe my feelings were not one-sided. But then I saw you with those girls. They are your type, Jared, and I am not.

"What type?"

"The perfect one. Tall, slim, impeccable looks. The way I always wanted to be."

I can feel the blush creeping up my cheeks.

Jared steps closer to me.

"Those women are anything but perfect.In the past... Those women were only good for getting laid and then kicked out of my house, which I'm not proud of, but that's what they were. Those women," he sighs, "aren't real, Hartley. You are!"

"Sorry, I felt like you were giving me mixed signals."

"Are you afraid of being with me because of Brody?" he asks suddenly, causing me to take a step back.

"What about Meghan?" I ask back, and he tenses up.

"I... I'm not perfect; I screwed up a lot. I thought I knew what I was doing, but I am apparently not doing a good job if you still don't get it."

"Get what, Jared?"

"That I'm fucking crazy about you," he shouts. At least, I think he is shouting.

My heart is pounding, and I can feel the cold raindrops on my face. Jared gasps, as do I, and then he grabs my waist and pulls me to him.

"Say it, Hartley. Say you want me as much as I want you, and I swear I'll give you the whole fucking world."

"God... Do you really have to ask?" the corner of my mouth twitches into a smile. Jared's lips fall to mine like a starved animal. His mouth tastes of rain and beer, and it's perfect.

His fingers dig deep into my hair, pulling my head back. I give in to his every move. He invites my tongue into a slow, deep dance, and I almost moan sharply at the intense sensation of his wet, hard body pressing me against his, kissing me senseless.

His hands make a bold move, grabbing my butt and effortlessly lifting me up. I instinctively wrap my legs around his waist, holding on as he carries us towards the door.

His lips brush the line of my jaw, and he gently scrapes his teeth down the sensitive skin of my neck. He sucks at the tender spot under my ear like he's starving. Like he's starving for me.

I barely realize I'm in his house until his foot kicks in the bedroom door.

My senses sharpen despite the silence. He lays me softly against the mattress, hovering over me. I stare directly into his eyes, and suddenly, my world feels complete. I don't need to hear to know that his every movement reflects his words.

"I'm trying to be slow," he signs.

"I don't want slow. I just want you." I grab his hips with my legs and pull him closer. "Come on, Jared, don't be a gentleman."

I can see it in his face as he groans in appreciation, feel the vibration of his chest under my palm, and his heart pounding.

In a fraction of a second, he releases me from my clothes, the fine material brushing my skin and ending up on the floor. I remove his shirt next and caress his toned muscles. He is built like a Greek statue.

He unbuckles his belt with trembling fingers and pulls off the light jeans with a pained expression. Then, as he places them on either side of my head, his gaze softens.

"You are so beautiful," he says clearly. He traces a line of blush down my cheek with his fingers, down my neck to my collarbone.

"You're beautiful," I reply, running my fingers through his wavy hair. God, I've wanted to do this for so long.

He unhooks my bra, pulling it off. He watches me with a hungry look that should embarrass me but only makes me feel sexier. I pull my panties off with my foot, and when they get stuck, he laughs and pulls them off to help me. Then I look down at him, his true self, and I salivate and gasp for air.

He spreads my thighs with his knees and descends between them, exploring my breasts with his mouth. He rubs against me slowly, tantalizingly. Arching my back, I push my hips towards his, begging for more.

Then those perfect lips move down, down my stomach. When he settles between my legs, he leaves a trail of kisses down the inside of my thighs, both sides, as if he doesn't want to miss an inch, looking me in the eyes the whole time. Biting my lip, I watch as he finally begins to lick my center with slow, long strokes. The sensation forces me to throw my head back, moaning in pleasure. My fingers dig into his hair, urging him into a faster rhythm, but he maintains his slow, teasing pace. He sinks one of his fingers into my aching center, and my legs begin to shake with my impending orgasm. His tongue plunges into me with each stroke, deeper and deeper, and just as I'm about to reach my peak, he pulls back and climbs back on top of me.

"I want to be inside you the first time you come," he speaks as he signs, and even though it's not perfect, I understand.

He takes his wallet from his back pocket and searches for the foil. He grins as he reads it, then looks up at the ceiling as if saying thank you. He says something about it not being expired.

Then it happens. He slides his length through my arousal and when I feel his tip press against me, I lift my hips higher in an impatient movement. He slides himself into me slowly, stretching every inch as his fingers continue to caress my clit.

Oh God, it's been so long, and I still can't believe it's finally happening with Jared Zykov.

"Let me know if you want me to slow down," he signs.

Interesting. His sign language relating to sex is almost perfect. This guy...

"I don't want you to slow down," I groan.

And I mean it. Maybe I'm a masochist. I haven't been with a man for a long time, but I want this man to make me his without holding back. As soon as I'm comfortable with his width, he pulls his hips back, and with a deep thrust, fills me to the brink. I gasp in painful pleasure, as his fingers continue to rub my sensitive bundle of nerves. He buries his face in the crook of my neck, biting into my flesh with his teeth, sucking, then soothing the sting with his tongue. His movements get faster and faster, as he continues his deep and brutal pace. Reaching under me, he lifts my hips, hitting a point inside me that makes me see stars.

I wrap my fingers around his shoulders, dig my nails into his skin, and hold tight. He begins to move his hips in soft, slow circles; the pleasure is unlike anything I have experienced before. His touches, the scent of him, are all too much, and I can't hold on any longer. As I come apart around him, my body spasms with pleasure.

I can't hear the scream I let out, but he has shattered my world.

Jared thrusts a few more times, and when his body begins to shake, I know he's coming too. He collapses on top of me like he's just run a marathon.

Our bodies intertwine, exhausted but happy, and I can't help the smile of satisfaction that spreads across my face. After this night together, I'm sure I'll want more of him in every way possible.

When he leans up and looks at me with a similar grin, I know he feels the same.

Jared

There's something peaceful about cuddling in bed with the woman of your dreams after a night of pleasure. I've never felt that way before; even when things were good between Meghan and I.

In my previous relationships, good sex was a plus, but with Hartley, making love was everything. I could feel it in my soul with every fucking breath I took.

My fingers caressed Hartley's back as she snuggled against me like a kitten. We lie facing each other, the light from the table lamp allowing us to see each other's faces so we can talk.

She let out a shaky sigh and closed her eyes for a moment. When she looked back up at me, her eyes shone a more vivid green.

"I was with Brody before my accident." My hand stops on the small of her back, and she laughs softly. "Sorry, I'm not sure this is the right time to tell you about him."

"Tell me," I nudge.

"It was teenage love, but he had a dysfunctional family. I was never his priority, and I never lived up to his parents. There was a lot of pressure on him," she sighs. "It was so detrimental to our relationship that we had a huge fight the night of my accident. Then... we broke up."

"The night of your accident?"

"I left his house minutes before I drove off the road," she looks at me wide-eyed. "Brody... he thought it was his fault, and unfortunately, a lot of people did as well. I tried, to no avail, to convince him that it wasn't his fault, but it was too much for him. Ultimately, it was the last straw, and he left everything, including me, behind. But I don't regret what happened between us at the end because I know his life is happier without the pressure of his family. After the accident, he offered to pay for some of my hospital bills. He didn't have much money, but what he did have, he chose to spend on me; that's how bad he felt. I sent him a thank-you note once, but he never replied. Our relationship was entirely over.

"Do you... still love him?"

"No, I don't, and I ended it, but it wasn't easy."

I brush her hair out of her face.

"I've seen your blog and heard you sing. God, Hartley, you're amazing, you're talented, and I'm pissed that your injury kept you from doing things you love." As soon as I say it, I instantly regret it because I'm afraid I've touched a subject that is too sensitive.

"Ugh, why did I tell you the name of my blog?" she covers her face as she laughs.

"Hey," I pull her hands away. "Don't be shy in front of me. Should I remind you what we were doing a few hours ago?"

"Right, yeah, you saw my hidden side," she grins. "I used to love music and blogging, but I only started blogging more often after the accident. Anyway," she shakes her head. "I miss music, I won't deny it, and as soon as I get the chance to regain my hearing, I'm going to take it."

You'll get that chance sooner than you think, baby. Much sooner.

"I want you to play for me. I want to hear your voice when you sing," comes out of me.

"I'll give you a concert in the shower," she winks.

"Oh yes," I pull back and kiss her on the nose. "I like the sound of that idea."

She laughs ruefully, and I hate myself for spoiling the mood, but since she's shared a painful part of her past, I feel it's only fair to share a part of myself with her.

"Meghan... During my NHL career, was my only serious girlfriend, though it didn't last that long."

Hartley focuses on what I am saying with interest.

"At first, I thought she was different from the others, but she quickly got sucked into the world of glamor and money, even if it was just the surface. We always fought. When I wanted to be alone, she wanted to show me off in front of her friends in some fancy club. I hated that life with all my heart. I felt terrible when you said you'd seen the articles about me. I remembered what it was like to stand in front of my mother. I'll never forget the disappointed look on her face when I first came home from an away game... No mother wants to see pictures of her son with women in every city he travels to across the country, even if most of it was just the media was trying to spin that I was some 'playboy'. I could have been more discreet. When I was drafted, I got carried away with the possibilities. I'm not proud of it, but I have changed a lot since then. I was a hot-tempered, rude asshole, and I didn't act any differently with women. They wanted nothing from me but sex or money. I thought it was what I wanted too in the beginning. But I always felt wrong about it, and a part of me always wanted more" Hartley looks like she's imagining it, her expression tensing as I attempt to soothe her by running my fingers over her face. "I'm not like that anymore... I swear. I realized I didn't want to be that man after things ended with Meghan. I was lonely and wanted to find a normal girl, even though I knew it was tough with my lifestyle. At first, she seemed to be what I was looking for, but she showed her true colors in the end. Since then... I haven't been with anyone," I admit. "You're the first."

"What?"

"I knew it would take patience to find the right girl for me."

"You... are perfect, Jared."

"Hart. I don't want you to read any more about me. Please believe me, that was just an old part of me. I'm afraid you might judge me by it."

"I didn't mean to, Jared. I'm sorry if what I said hurt you."

"I probably wouldn't have come to a different conclusion if I were you," I snort. "I miss hockey, but I wouldn't go back. The fame, the media, it's all just a facade. Many of the guys cheat on their wives and then play the dutiful husband at home. It broke me. My spirit was too weak for that," I confessed. It wasn't the money and the victories that would make me forget. "I've been pretty hard on hockey since I was a kid, and maybe the reality of professional hockey took some of my love for the sport. I hope to find it again now that there are no restraining factors. The pressure in my chest thaws. I've been holding this in for a long time, and finally, having someone to share it with is priceless. I was afraid to admit my pain because all I got from everyone was, "Be thankful the NHL is putting all that money under your ass. Do you know how many people dream of being a professional hockey player?"

"Thank you for telling me," she strokes my jaw, and I lean in.

"And thank you for being you."

*

I grin as I make pancakes for breakfast while Hartley is still sleeping. I'm not ashamed to admit I had to run out last night to get a box of condoms and stayed up all night pleasing her.

Yesterday was almost perfect, despite the bar fight, the reopened wounds, and the tears. None of those things could take away from finally experiencing everything I have been fantasizing about doing with Hart.

We were up until three in the morning and had to leave for Moonlight soon, so I make a champion's breakfast to fill my girl's belly.

During our evening of amazing sex and sharing deeper parts of ourselves, we decided that we both wanted more than to be 'just friends'. I pause momentarily, reflecting on how great it feels to be able to call Hartley Knight my girlfriend. I turn around to hear soft footsteps and see her stumbling into the kitchen, sleepy and disheveled in my huge t-shirt. She sniffs the air sweetly.

"Good morning. I found some spinach and thought I'd make some veggie pancakes. I fried some bacon, too," I said, pointing to the pile of meat with my spatula.

"The perfect guy makes a perfect breakfast," she says as she approaches me. I grab her shirt and pull her to me. Come here," I say as I kiss her slowly. "Hi, Poppy."

"That's my name now, is it?" Then her eyes go to the vase. "You picked poppies again. Did you get any sleep?"

"I'll be fine, that's what I get for keeping you up until dawn," I wink at her. When I turn back to the counter, I suddenly freeze. A strange feeling rushes through me before I hear the rumble of a loud engine.

I turn to see Hartley watching me in confusion.

I hear a door slam, the heavy thud of boots on the porch, and a knock.

"Hey, asshole, open the door!"

"No fucking way!"

Hartley

I'm still groggy, but reality hits me hard. I just spent a whole night with Jared Zykov.

The guy who I, at first, thought was an idiotic jerk. Then I doubted I could meet his standards, which wounded my pride a bit more than I care to admit.

And now I'm standing in Candace's kitchen, staring at fresh poppies, spinach pancakes, and crispy bacon towers.

Holy shit! I slept with Candace's grandson!

Jared leaves the kitchen and heads to the front door, opening it with a heavy sigh. I only grasp the reason for his shift in mood when I see the grinning young guy standing on the porch.

He's a bit shorter than Jared and has a slimmer build. He is wearing a dark blue shirt, which reads "Best Russian Quality" in parentheses. His dark hair is messy, and his black sunglasses cover half his face. He gives Jared a thousand-watt grin and says, "I'm home!"

He abruptly pulls Jared into a bear hug while Jared stares at him, still confused.

As soon as he sees me, he pushes Jared away so hard that he falls against the wall. He stares wide-eyed, and as he moves toward me, he removes his glasses. His eyes... wow. I've never seen gray eyes before.

"And who are you, my beauty?"

I let out a small laugh, not at Jared, who angrily grabs the back of the guy's head and pulls him back.

"Hartley, this monkey is my brother," he signs but also speaks as the surprise visitor looks at him nervously.

Jared walks over to me, finds the notepad, and writes Sawyer on it. I wouldn't know it by the way he moves his lips. I have trouble with names.

"What are you doing?" Sawyer looks at us suspiciously.

"Speak clearly. Hartley can't hear you," he replies so I can see his face.

Sawyer's eyes dart between us in surprise, then he pulls his lips into a broad grin, and when I see the long dimples, I see the real resemblance between them.

"Well," he walks over to me and takes my hand. "My pleasure," he kisses the back of my hand.

"Wow, your brother is a real gentleman."

"Don't believe him," Jared signs.

"What did you tell her? Bro, that's not fair. You can talk to me anytime." I think he says something like that.

"Speak fucking slower. She reads lips."

"Sure, I'm at a disadvantage because you're signing?"

I laugh, loud and hearty, and they stare at me with wide eyes. Sawyer turns to his brother, pleased.

"I get it now. You've got my full support for your relationship!"

Jared and Sawyer talk alone in the kitchen while I run next door to shower and change. When I'm sufficiently refreshed, I meet Jared at the Jeep.

We drive to the Moonlight together, and although we have trouble communicating while driving, he tells me in the parking lot that Sawyer was sent here by his grandmother to get some time off from work. He says she wants her grandson to rediscover his passion for creating, and the Moonlight project can help him do that.

"I'll support it as long as it doesn't interfere with my work!" I reply, jokingly.

Jared laughs, then takes my hand as we walk to the front door. This makes me stop.

"What do we do now?"

We haven't discussed exactly what will happen today, and I feel we need to do that before we go to work. He looks down at me with a soft smile.

"I don't want to hide, but we can be discreet in there if you want. I wouldn't want you to have a problem with anyone."

I think my heart stops for a moment.

"Okay... I mean, we'll be careful?"

"Whatever you are comfortable with, you're my girl," he shakes his head, laughing. "Baby, you can tell me anything. In fact, I always want you to tell me what you're thinking.

When a man asks me to do that, he doesn't know what he's getting into, but I accept.

We let go of each other's hands in the lobby, but after we swipe our cards and I head for the creative department, he's still on my tail.

"Where are you going?"

"I'll walk you," he looks at me innocently as I raise an eyebrow. "Okay, okay, I was hoping for a little sneaky smooch in that dark cubicle by the door."

I swear it's like we're still teenagers. But that doesn't stop me from pulling him into the corner, from which I emerge a few minutes later with swollen lips and disheveled hair.

*

Before lunch, I stop by the North Wing, where the decorators have already begun implementing my plans.

The twisted columns are still in the works. My living snow globe inspiration, a wall of snowflakes floating in front of a painted backdrop, is being installed as I arrive. I stomp around excitedly as my fellow technicians light up the interactive wall. The Moonlight Tourist Center is a gateway to the world in our town, entertaining people with different themes each season. It's like a castle entrance that leads to various fairy tale worlds. For me, the fall and winter styles are my absolute favorites. I get excited when I imagine tourists taking a break at this place and walking along the wobbly forest path behind the castle, between the mountains and the forest.

I always look forward to snow, cold, and the aesthetic winter carnival. I can add that to McRoyal's very small list of positive choices.

My mouth waters as I picture the almond hot chocolate and the vanilla custard in the pistachio wafers, both staples at the winter carnival.

"So, did you have a good night?" signs Eric as he touches my side. "Jared's seems to be in some sort of mood."

"I have no idea what you are talking about," I ask, trying to hide the blush that I can feel warming my face.

"He's a rabid lion," he snorts. "I can feel the tension between the two of you."

"There is nothing going on with Jared and me," I smile cheekily at him, then he grabs my arm, eyes wide, and pulls me aside.

"You have to tell me everything! I have to know before Jenna does."

Too late... She video called me this morning while I was getting dressed at my place, wanting to know every sordid detail.

He catches the slight cringe on my face. "Oh great, I'm last one to find out again."

"We're just... enjoying each other's company."

"Please tell me what he's like in bed. Is it tender, or is he the typical cute guy who gives it to you hard?"

"Can you at least speak slowly so I can understand what you're saying," I blow a stray strand of hair out of my face.

"Please don't deprive me of this information."

"He was sweet, okay? But when I asked him not to hold back..."

"I knew it! Jared isn't as innocent as he seems," he grins.

Taking my phone out of my pocket when I feel it vibrate, Eric keeps going on about how happy he is for me to finally get laid. After a while, I tune out his words and what he is signing to me and focus solely on the email displayed on my screen. I had to read it three times to fully grasp its content. When I finally look up, Eric's concerned gaze meets mine.

"Are you okay?" he signs.

"You don't have to sign anymore," I say, dazed.

"What?"

"I said you don't have to sign anymore."

Then, I walk away, leaving him in confusion.

Jared

Sawyer spins like a child in my chair as he surveys the small office where I don't really work. I just keep all the paperwork for the projects and occasionally negotiate with buyers or producers who help Moonlight with various things.

My brother rubs his chin as he surveys the area, then looks at me questioningly.

"I always thought you were an important person, someone to be taken seriously. Yet here you are, monkeying around in a suit, bossing people around."

I look down at my worn jeans and red flannel shirt.

"I'm not some shark behind a desk, I take my involvement in this project very seriously."

"Yeah, yeah, but you're the lead investor."

Sometimes, I wonder if my brother has lost his mind from all the fights we had as kids, teenagers, and maybe even now.

"So... Grandma sent you here to rediscover your long-lost creativity."

"Yeah."

"To me, in Alaska."

"Yeah."

"For the Moonlight Project."

"Hey, let's not try to decipher her intentions just yet. We'll understand what's going on once we're finished with the project, and until then, we have two new assignments she's given us."

"Okay, then make yourself useful and walk around the creative department. See if anything inspires you," I say, pointing at his chest.

"Nothing's inspired me in a while," he mumbles.

I'm about to ask what the hell's wrong with him when someone bursts into the office without knocking. Hartley runs towards me, and before I know it, she's jumping at me, sending me staggering backward. Sawyer raises an eyebrow.

"So that's why you got an office, bro. A little workplace hanky-panky?"

I ignore him because Hartley can't hear anyway. As she slides off my body, she plants a hard kiss on my lips, and I look at her in surprise.

"You won't believe what happened?" she jumps up and down.

"Okay, Poppy, calm down," I laugh and grab her hand to stop her from falling backward.

"I got an email from the clinic that is about 45 minutes outside of town. Dr. Jacobson, a prominent New York doctor, will be passing through, and he's taken some patients from Dr. Declan's list. You won't believe who made it to the top of the list. Me," she exclaims. "Me, Jared. I am going to get my surgery."

"Wow, Hart... that's fantastic!"

"I have to go in on Wednesday for an exam and a consultation. They said it would be quick, but since Dr. Jacobson won't be staying long, his partner will be doing the post-op follow-ups," she said excitedly. "I can't believe it. I might... hear again. Jared, I'm going to hear your voice," she looks at me with a huge twinkle in her eyes.

My face is stinging, and my heart is racing. Is that's what she truly wants? She didn't say she wants to hear music; she wants to hear my voice.

"You're going to hear again," I squeeze her hand. "Dr. Jacobson is the best. I mean... he has to be the best if he's from New York." God, I'm such an idiot. Fortunately, Hartley is so excited that she ignores my stumble.

Sawyer looks at me suspiciously.

"Yeah, that's interesting, Jared. A doctor who's impossible to get into decides to come here willingly. That's quite a miracle," he says, pursing his lips. If he says anything else, I might punch him in the face. My palms are tingling. Hartley steps back, wiping her hands on her jeans, in which her butt looks fantastic.

"Will you come with me? To the consultation?"

"Really?" I step back toward her. "Yeah, fuck, of course I will go with you."

"But only if you don't mind. I know you have to work..."

"There is nothing that could stop me from going, Hart!"

Sawyer gets up from my chair, jumps over to Hartley, and wraps his arm around her neck.

"Congratulations, beautiful! Don't worry, I'll take over your creative duties."

Hartley looks at me pleadingly, and I let out a small laugh.

"Jared said I should check out the creative department," he shouts, and I slap him hard on the back of the head.

"I said she can't hear you, you idiot. Yelling doesn't help her understand."

"I'm going back to work," Hart crawls out from under my brother's arm, clapping her hands excitedly.

"Hey, wait, I'm serious," Sawyer yells after her, following her down the hall.

I wonder for a second if he's actually my brother or if my parents found him in a dumpster...

I plop down on the small couch across from the desk and call my old coach. My heart is still pounding with excitement.

"Jared, what's up?" he calls, and the noises in the background are all too familiar. The sound of skating and screaming makes me smile. I am about to experience it all over again, only from the coaching side.

"Sorry to interrupt, Coach Cole."

"Practice just ended. I'm coaching some spoiled brats this month." I can just picture him tearing his hair out and yelling at them. "Were you able to get in touch with the doctor?"

"Yeah, Dr. Jacobson is flying in. I'll never be able to repay your kindness."

"It's no problem. I promised to help however I could, and I'm a man of my word. Have you considered my offer, or have you decided to stay in Alaska?"

"Unfortunately, I can't accept. It's a great opportunity, and I sure you will find someone to fill the spot. I'm... I'm fine. I'm more than fine. I'm going to lead a damn weak team to victory," I grin. Although I have yet to see the high school team play, which will happen in August, the info I do have about the team is not encouraging.

"That's the Jared I know. He'd rather help those who need it than work with the pros again," he laughs. "If you ever change your mind, I'll be here, but I hope you don't. I hear you're doing better than ever. Oh, and say hello to the girl. I hope the operation goes well."

"How did you..."

"I doesn't take rocket science to figure out that you wouldn't fly a world-famous doctor to a remote city in Alaska for just anyone," he says with a chuckle.

"I'm sure there are other doctors could do it, but I wanted the best!

"And Cage's big mouth told me everything."

That asshole. I miss Cage, and we haven't spoken much lately, but when we spoke last, I filled him in on everything going on here in Alaska.

"The team misses you, especially him. You know he's retiring at the end of the season. He would never admit it, but he could use some support".

"I've already invited a few of the guys to come out for a visit," I sigh. "I hope they can make it out soon. I invited Cage, Jason, and his wife, Marleen." They were the closest to me at home.

"It will be good for them."

Considering Jason was traded to Vancouver next season, I am sure a vacation would be greatly appreciated.

I talked to him for a few more minutes to hear about the team and its new lineup, making sure to take notes in case I can use something when I'm coaching.

When Coach starts yelling at the kids, who are hitting each other with wet towels, I let him go and say goodbye.

I rest my head on the couch and sigh with satisfaction. For once, I finally feel like everything is going to work out perfectly.

Hartley

If I thought that Boyle was the biggest public enemy on the creative them, I stand corrected. Sawyer came in today like royalty and dove straight into work.

"In the East Wing, take out most of the Far Eastern culture and bring in more of the Middle East, like Turkish and Arabic cultures."

How are we going to implement all of his changes this close to opening?

Thankfully, the South and West Wings got away with some minor nitpicking. When we made it to the North Wing, he started making jokes about how cool it would be to change the design to be inspired by the movie Santa Claus or Krampus, I threatened to send him to the North Pole myself.

When Jared heard my outburst, he laughed all the way to the clinic, and my heart ached because I wanted to finally hear his laugh. But soon—soon, everything would change.

Now, he sits with me as promised, holding my hand under the table.

"We're going to do some routine tests before the procedure to ensure everything is going well," Dr. Jacobson says.

I'm already planning how to manage my time off and how to work from home during my recovery without compromising the Moonlight project.

"Tympanoplasty is a routine procedure in our clinic; we perform it under anesthesia. It can be local or general, depending on the perforation. We rebuild the tympanic membrane. It may also be necessary to reconstruct small bones in the ear. We make an incision in the ear canal or behind the ear and perform the procedure through that incision."

"How long is the recovery time?" asks Jared, trying to sign despite struggling with the subject. I mostly read his lips. "Is there anything we can do or prepare at home to make her recovery easier?" He squeezes my hand again as if he needs more support.

"I read that she will have to wear a bandage for two weeks. And I'm assuming she'll have to stay home and rest, right? Making sure Hartley does nothing but rest won't be easy, but I'll do my best.".

I can't decide whether to kick him in the butt or kiss him for looking into all this.

"Some people feel comfortable enough to return to normal activities after a week, but it varies. I recommend 2 weeks of rest at a minimum.

Alternatively, I recommend using noise-reduction earplugs initially because the high and shrill sounds can be distracting. You will also be given an antibiotic medication to take for one week following the procedure."

"Okay, that's encouraging," Jared nods and smiles at me.

"We can do it next Monday if that works for you."

"And if it doesn't?" Jared asks back.

"I'm only asking out of courtesy. You don't have much of a choice if you want to avoid waiting longer because I'm flying back in two weeks," the doctor says, looking at Jared blankly. "I will prepare the paperwork during the tests and get back to you on Thursday with a final procedure summary."

When the doctor leaves us, Jared turns to me with an excited look on his face.

"You're going to be fine, Poppy."

"I know."

"Should I ask him how long after the procedure it is recommended to not have sex?" he asks earnestly, and I look at him in disbelief.

"You are beyond redemption..."

*

I left Jared and Sawyer alone for some man time and decided to walk over to my cabin to make them a surprise dinner. I haven't spent much time in the kitchen since the Moonlight Project started, but I'm making up for it now.

On Sunday, I bought fresh fruit, blueberries, and strawberries to make a sauce for my homemade cheesecake.

For my main course, I'm making a truffle risotto with parmesan that's so creamy it melts in your mouth.

I'm starting with a chicken and vegetable base and Jenna's dad's aged white wine. I stir in a big dollop of grated parmesan and butter. As it simmers in the pan, I give it a good stir.

The boys arrive shortly after I finish the sauce and I can see them pushing each other as they walk toward the house from the window. Sawyer slaps Jared on the back of the head, pushing his brother into the prickly bush.

Oh my God... I thought my brother was a dick.

Jared comes in the door and grins as he sniffs the air and clutches at his chest as if he is in pain.

"Something really cheesy going on, huh?"

"Parmesan risotto with truffles. And cheesecake," I point to the ingredients. "But I haven't started yet, so you can help me with that."

Sawyer dusts off his pants and steps in after his brother, watching Jared like a bloodhound on the hunt for revenge.

I have the boys to work in less than ten minutes, partly because I don't want them eating the risotto before it's done and partly because I want to form a barricade between them before it gets out of hand.

On one side of me, Jared mixes the mascarpone cream while I crush graham crackers for the base. On the other side of me, Sawyer is busy mashing fruit with a spoon, but I don't tell him that the blender is about a foot away.

They eye each other as they work, and after a while, I notice that they're competing against each other.

"Look at this, Hartley," Jared points to the cream as he works on it with outstretched arms. I think he's even flexing his bicep a little. Sawyer taps me on the arm.

"Um, Hartley," Sawyer turns to me. He is blending the fruit so aggressively that I'm afraid he's going to splatter it all over the nice furniture. "Look how well I'm doing. That's good, right?"

I look at Jared.

"What's wrong with your brother?"

"Don't mind him. He fell on his head as a kid and hasn't been right since."

I should have just ordered a pizza.

Jared

Hartley's family was in complete panic when their daughter shared the news. They're anticipating the results of the tests Hartley will have done this week and will be at the hospital with us on Monday. They planned to celebrate by inviting us for a barbecue this weekend.

Her mother made a veiled comment that she would love to finally be introduced to the secret admirer the whole town was talking about.

Wanting to impress both her and her daughter, I asked Hartley to help me brush up on my sign language.

"I still don't understand how you learned so much, so fast," she says incredulously.

It's a cold and stormy day, so I asked her to stay the night. Now we sit across from each other in front of the fireplace as she teaches me to new sentences to sign.

"I took a short course online," I confess, embarrassed. "And in the evening, I go to a class in town."

Hartley stares at me, stunned.

"So that's where you disappear to at night? Jared... that's..." She shakes her head and begins to sign.

"Thank you!"

"You're welcome." I smile.

"I'm going to show you a few things I have learned," I reply, "correct me if I'm wrong."

"I like you! Very much," I sign. "You have such pretty eyes."

"Okay, you have compliments mastered," she laughs, tilting her head to the side as she bites her lip. "I like you too. And you have nice eyes too."

"I think about you all the time," I reply. "Your mouth always tastes like..." How do you sign cinnamon? I point to her coffee cup, and she laughs, showing me the signs for coffee and cinnamon. "Your mouth always tastes of cinnamon."

"Because I always drink cinnamon coffee," she replies with a smile.

"You're sooooo sweet," comes an unwelcome voice. Under the archway of the living room, Sawyer stands leaning against the wall, a steaming mug in his hand.

"Fuck off, Saw!"

"Are you learning to sign?"

"Yeah."

"Can I come in?" he asks excitedly. No way.

"Sawyer, I'm sorry, but do you have anything else to do?" I ask, looking at him meaningfully, but he shrugs.

"No. But why? Am I interrupting your date?" he grins.

I stand up slowly and stretch.

"I'll give you ten seconds to run."

"What happened to a thirty second head start, dude?" he asks, setting his cup down on the dresser.

"You lost that when you ruined my date."

"But this is my house, too!" he exclaims. "Half yours, half mine."

"But I rent it! And what part does Brianna get?"

"She loves the yard."

"You've got half a second!"

Then Sawyer jumps up and slaps me.

"You jerk!" he laughs, but before he can run away, I pull his legs out from under him and slam him to the ground. He screams like a child as I push his hands to the ground.

"Guys, stop it," Hartley yells. "You're like children."

God forbid I lose this woman because my wretched brother brings out the worst in me.

"Will you leave us alone for the rest of our lives and get off my back?" I ask my captive brother.

"You think you can take me down just because you're a hockey god? Like I said, I have as much right to be here as you do!"

"You admit I'm a hockey god? Did hell freeze over?"

"Hey, guys! Break it up right now!" Hartley stomped past me.

"Yeah, let's stop. Everybody go to your own room," Sawyer nods. "I'll take the big room; you take the guest room."

"Fucking dream on."

"Hartley!" the idiot yells. "If you don't stop him, he'll do it!"

"What are you going to do?" she asks me.

"He's drooling on me."

"Ew..."

I snort.

"It's coming. You want long and thin or the tried and true thick?"

Sawyer grins, then flashes a very deep malice in his eyes.

"Asshole!" he yells in my face and kicks me in the ass so hard it hits my balls.

I crouch to the side, grabbing my groin. Jesus Christ, that feels like hell.

Sawyer runs off, and Hartley leans over me like an angel. She calls worriedly, but my ears are beeping, and I can't hear. Her gaze darkens and she goes after my brother. After what seems like an agonizingly long time, she pulls him out by the ear, and I am overwhelmed with satisfaction.

"Apologize!" she commands Sawyer.

"But he started it," he groans in pain, but Hart tugs on his ear. "Okay, okay, sorry!"

"Now. You're both going to go into the kitchen, sit on opposite sides of the table, and you're not getting up until you make peace."

She's so hot when she's angry. Too bad I'm at death's door, because I'd kiss her senseless right now.

*

Something is wrong with my brother.

Aside from the fact that we are always fighting, I know that something is wrong. I don't believe that Grandma sent him here just to get break from his life. If that were the case, she would have driven me here a long time ago. Grandma won't tell me anything;

she insists that what she says to the grandchildren stays between us, and I respect that about her.

After the storm cleared later that evening, I headed into town to grab a nice bottle of wine for tomorrow's dinner, as a gift for Hartley's family and her brother. I am hoping we can make amends; we didn't have the best interaction the first time we met, and I'd like to make it up to him. The last thing I needed was to have Hartley's brother and the whole town on my case if I messed up.

Now I'm second-guessing and praying that Sawyer doesn't unsettle Hart too much. Like interfering with her plans outside of work.

On my music list I have Slipknot, Gojira, Led Zeppelin, but this time I chose Alice Cooper. As I turn the corner, the wine starts to roll off of the seat, I reach to catch it just in time as I steer with one hand and swerve to the left. Damn it, I'm balancing life and death like a circus monkey. I jerk the wheel just in time to avoid a crash with car in the other lane, then come to a sharp stop on the side of the road with a loud slam of my brakes.

Flashing lights appear behind me.

"What the hell? How the hell did the cops get here so fast?"

I must be having a streak of bad luck. I bang my head on the steering wheel a few times and wait for the Judgment Squad to arrive. In the rearview mirror I see an officer get out of the car and walk toward me with slow, firm steps. I push the wine back into the bag and straighten up. I roll down the window and am confronted by a dark-haired man in his fifties. He leans against the car and looks at me questioningly.

"Good evening!" I force a smile.

"Good evening. Is there a problem? The roads around here are pretty slippery. Where are you headed?"

"I'm renting a cabin on the lake."

"Then you should have taken the north road; it's a shorter drive."

"There is a north road?"

He laughs softly.

"Tourist, huh?"

"My grandmother has lived here for as long as I can remember, but yes... I'm a tourist," I sigh.

"Well, if you turn off here, you can go up and save about ten minutes. This road is more commonly used by ATV riders heading into the woods to bang around in the mud."

"All right, thanks!"

Then, as if some higher power is trying to make fun of me, the damn bottle pops out of the paper bag again, as if to wave, "hello, I'm here".

The officer looks at me suspiciously, raising an eyebrow.

"Well, that's a different story."

"I haven't been drinking!" I exclaim. "I'm bringing this as a gift, it-it just keeps falling out..."

"In that case, if you don't mind," he pulls out a breathalyzer. "Please blow into this."

"I... My girlfriend made risotto and used wine in it. Can you detect that?"

"I doubt the boiled wine she used in the risotto would count in this situation," he says, pursing his lips.

I let out a tired sigh and blow on the probe. I smile in satisfaction when it gives no indication.

"Please don't risk your life or the lives of others over a bottle of wine. I doubt a bottle of wine is worth that much."

If you knew I thought my girlfriend's brother was her lover when I first met him, you wouldn't say that.

"Of course I understand, sir."

"Oh, and we are looking forward to having you over for dinner tomorrow, Jared."

My entire body freezes, and I slowly look at the man who is staring at me with a smirk etched across his face. Oh, fuck me...

"Mr. Knight?"

"It's a pleasure to finally meet you, son. I hope you'll drive more cautiously with my daughter beside you, though."

"I swear, it's never happened before," I apologize. "I can assure you, sir, your daughter's safety is my top priority."

138

"Tomorrow then!" he slams the roof of my car.

Well, this is fantastic! I meet my girl's dad for the first time, and he gives me a hard time because he thinks I've been drinking and driving, all because of a near mishap over a bottle of wine.

He must have a pretty high opinion of me now.

Hartley

I grab the paleo cookie tray while Jared unloads the drinks from the car. I had to bake an extra bowl of cookies because the first batch was gone before we even left the house. These two men are like two big hungry kids.

"I still can't believe my dad made you do that," I laugh.

"I hope I can make it up to him with wine," he raises the bottle that is to blame for his abrupt meeting with my father last night.

"At this rate, you'll soon be his adopted son," Sawyer taps him on the shoulder. "Do you understand me, Hartley?"

"You don't always have to ask. If you talk too fast, I'll tell you."

We stroll down the narrow path alongside my family's house to the garden, where my mother has already arranged the large wooden table. She's whipped up a variety of Turkish dishes from Grandma's recipe book. Turkish women swear the way to a man's heart is through his stomach, and with Mom's cooking, Jared and Sawyer will be putty in her hands. I'm betting on it.

When we arrive, Mom greets us with a big smile and gives each of us a big hug. I introduce the boys to her, and she looks at them with satisfaction.

"Good choice, darling. He has very good genes," She signs with a smirk.

"Mom, stop!"

"What did she say?" asks Jared curiously.

"I'm not going to tell you because it will just add to your already massive ego," I sigh.

I've purposely chosen to wear my poppy red dress. It's cute, short length makes it impossible for Jared to tear his eyes away from my glistening thighs, so I consider my choice a success.

"Jared, Sawyer, I'm so glad you're here. You can call me Hande, not Mrs. Knight—Hande. You know, just keeping myself young," she says, signing gracefully. Her sign language is so elegant that I often find myself a bit jealous of her.

I get my long, curly hair from her, and her green eyes, but my features are more like my father's, who just stepped out from behind the grill.

"There you are Hartley. Hello, Jared and this must be your brother?"

"Sawyer, sir. I brought you a gift, premium Russian vodka. I would know, we are Russian," he holds up the bottle. "And you should know I don't drink and drive," he winks.

I guess Jared won't be hearing the end of that anytime soon.

"I know a bit about your heritage from your grandmother," my father twirls the drink in his hand. "I had a friend who was also Russian. We drank so much vodka once that I spent the night in a ditch. Your mother sent the police after me. She thought I had run away before the wedding.

"Sir, I'd love to hear all about your drunken escapades. It's not every day you get to hear them from a police commissioner," Sawyer nods.

"Call me Mick. I'm off duty tonight, let's open this and pour ourselves some drinks," he grins. "Jared? Hope the wine made the trip."

Everyone laughs, and I squeeze his hand in encouragement.

"My dad likes you," I sign. "He only jokes with people he likes."

"Your dad must be pretty brave to get that drunk before the big day," I stifle a laugh.

"If you only knew how many stories he has," I mutter under my breath. Stories about me and my brother. I just hope they don't come out today.

"What a meal," Sawyer exclaims, staring wide-eyed at the table. "This is a true cultural feast."

"I made burek and baklava, because that's usually popular with people trying Turkish food for the first time," my mother begins. "We're making lamb on the grill to stuff into homemade pita. And I also made ayran. Have you ever had ayran?"

Jared and Sawyer shake their heads. The familiar look of challenge of ensuring guests leave with full bellies, is evident in my mother's determined gaze. But with these two men, it won't be a difficult task at all.

Caleb arrives with a bouquet of flowers to sweep Mom off her feet. He totally stole that from my dad.

Jared stretches out next to me, clearing his throat and hands my brother the wine meant for him. I don't know if that's why he bought so many drinks, because he wants to get into their hearts by getting them drunk. My brother's eyes light up, so I guess he's on the right track.

"Hey, man. I am sorry about my behavior the other day."

"No problem. I'd be jealous too if I thought the girl I was crazy about was sleeping around."

"What?" says Mom, and they both say nothing.

"Thanks," he takes the wine, then suddenly frowns. "But if you hurt my sister, I hope you know what will happen."

"I know, I know, you'll punch me in the face."

"But only if you deserve it."

"How nice of you..." I murmur.

Someone covers my eyes, and I feel the touch of a cold hand on my cheek. When I turn around, I see Jenna's grinning face.

"Hello, my little dwarf," she looks over at us and kisses my cheek. "Jared," she nods to him.

"Jenna, we haven't talked since you hit on me outside the bar."

"We talked at the ball, you asshole."

"Really?"

"Yeah, I threatened you to be nice to my best friend."

"You small towners really like to threaten."

I scratch my head nervously, hoping they don't start a fight. Sawyer who is seated next to Jared, leans around Jared and I to talk to Jenna. She stares at the chattering boy with such concern that I begin to feel sorry for him.

When no one is threatening anyone and no more embarrassing stories are being told, my father serves the smoky lamb chops, and we begin to eat. I try to pay attention to the others, because my family is signing a lot to make it easier for me to understand the conversation. Remembering that soon, this will no longer be necessary, and the nervousness in my stomach grows.

What if the procedure fails for some reason? If I go to the clinic believing that I will soon be able to hear again and it doesn't work, it would be devastating. There's nothing worse than soaring up high, only to have your wings torn off and crash. Maybe my biggest fear is flying low.

Jared squeezes my hand, and I turn to him.

"Are you okay?" he asks, signing.

"I was just thinking."

The food is delicious, but everyone's favorite is baklava. My mother hands me the ayran and I pour it into my glass. Opening a soda bottle, I pour some onto the aryan. The guys look at me curiously, as they sip the yogurt on its own.

"What are you doing?" asks Sawyer.

"Look at that, Hartley's quite the rebel. Only a few of my Turkish friends drink ayran like that."

"Show me," Jared nudges curiously.

"Nothing fancy about it," I laugh. "You pour the ayran, then you pour the soda." I put the spoon in. "Then you stir it well."

"I'll try," Sawyer takes the soda from me and adds it to his cup.

I make a quiet moan as I drink it; it's so refreshing. I grin at Jared, who also mixes his Ayran with soda, and firmly nod.

Sawyer gags, but Jared seems to enjoy the combination.

"I'll make coffee and tea," Mom gets up, and I help her pack up some of the dirty dishes. My brother follows us and gets my attention.

"Shall we go for a walk? I want to talk to you," he nods towards the street.

"Sure, let's go. Are you okay?"

"I'm fine. I just wanted to see if you're okay."

Jared

Hart and Caleb are out for a walk, and the others are chatting over a cup of coffee or tea. My brother left a few minutes ago with a bottle of beer in his hand, and I decided to follow him.

I found him at the end of the garden. He is looking at the landscape while taking a big gulp of beer.

"Hey," I come up next to him. "Everything okay?"

"Yeah, it was an amazing meal," he grins.

"Sawyer, what's up with you?"

He watches you with a slight smile on his face.

"What do you mean?"

"I know that when you get all huffy and puffy, you're trying to distract yourself from something. I can see it in your face. Something's driving you crazy. Did something happen?"

"Jared, no!"

"Saw..."

He turns to me, his expression one of determination.

"Not now, okay? I'll be fine, I just have a little problem at work. Don't worry about that now; worry about Hartley. You have a big day on Monday."

"You'll tell me everything afterward." It wasn't a question; it was a statement.

"Did you know that you're my favorite in the family? I love everybody, but you're the one person I would go to without question if I had a problem. I just need to digest things before discussing them. In the meantime, I'm going to kick your ass a few more times, and all will be right with the world."

I ruffle his hair hard.

"I won't fight you in front of my girl's dad. I don't need to go to jail for assault." I don't think Hartley wants to visit one, either.

"Fine, but I can kick your ass at home, right? Just once?"

As we made our way back to the group, I pushed him hard into a pine tree and gave him what he wanted.

He catches up quickly, picking off bits of the plant himself.

"Hey," he grabs my arm. "Did you tell Hartley yet?"

Shit. I know what he's referring to; my brother's not stupid.

"Not yet."

"When are you going to tell her you called the doctor to come here?"

"I'll tell her, not yet. After her surgery, I will."

"Your secret's under lock and key," he jests, miming the action of sealing his lips, locking them, and tossing away the imaginary key.

"You better. She needs to hear it from me."

"I'm going to find the bathroom."

Sawyer runs after Hande as she enters the house and takes the dishes from her. I hear a throaty sound behind me and suddenly turn around.

Jenna looks at me, stunned, and I know she heard everything.

"Jenna..."

"No, stop! Just answer my question, okay? Did you really do it?"

My shoulders sag as I sigh.

"Yes."

"You... Jared, it's..." she presses her lips together. "I can't find the words."

"Please don't tell her. I want to tell her."

"When?"

"How about when we're at the hospital, and she's being wheeled into surgery? I'm sure she won't be able to yell at me then."

"Jesus, Jared!"

"I'll tell her after the surgery. I want her to hear it from me, okay?"

"Okay, I won't tell her," she crosses her arms and looks at me mysteriously. "I misjudged you. I thought you couldn't be trusted, that you would take what you wanted from Hartley and then leave her with a broken heart, but I was wrong."

"Yeah?"

Jenna nods.

"You love Hartley," she explains. "Only someone in love would do what you have done. I have no idea how to thank you for helping her. If you ever need a kidney, please let me know."

"What condition are they in?" I smile.

"I have beautiful kidneys."

"I bet you do," I laugh.

Hartley

"I hope this isn't about Jared."

"He's a good guy, but I'm still a little confused about our first meeting," he replies, signing all the while.

"Did you know Dad already met him? He gave him a talking-to because he thought he was driving drunk."

Caleb laughs with his head thrown back.

"The Knight family doesn't make it easy."

We don't talk for a while; we walk and enjoy the rays of the setting sun. Caleb is quiet, but I can tell he has something on his mind.

He nudges my shoulder.

"I know what's bothering you, sis. You're afraid of change, which is normal and understandable. But it's going to be okay. I checked with the doctor, and he's the best. I still don't understand what he's doing here in Alaska, but there's nothing to worry about."

"Thanks, Caleb, I needed to hear that," I reflect. "I'm always trying to be strong, but truth be told, I'm exhausted, you know?"

"I understand, Hartley. I'm tired of being strong all the time, too, and having to protect you," he grins as I nudge him in the side.

"I never needed it."

"You don't, but I do. I love being the big brother."

I chuckle to myself, and I see a familiar face when I look up. Tara, our neighbor's daughter, stops in front of us and looks at me with interest. I had no idea she was home.

"Hi."

"Hi, Tara," Caleb nods at her. "What's up?"

"Not much, just visiting my parents. What about you guys? I hear you'll be back to normal soon," she says, casting me a tight-lipped smile. "You must be looking forward to living a full life again. It's not fashionable to feel sorry for yourself anymore." Caleb stretches next to me. "Oh, sorry, that was rude. I mean, nobody likes to be pitied." To her credit, she's out of her mind and has no idea she's insulting me.

"Tara, shut up," Caleb says, and by the look on his face, he's just using his quiet, angry tone.

"Okay, that came out wrong. I mean, it's tough to build relationships like that; not everyone's willing or able to adapt to someone who..."

"Who, what?" I ask, and a blush comes all over her face. "Tara, consider what you're saying. Not that it's any of your business. I'm not some attention-seeking person with a disability like you're making me out to be. But for what it's worth, I have a strong support system and a boyfriend who is happy to be with me regardless of my hearing loss."

She covers her mouth, and I walk back to the house, dragging Caleb behind me. My brother stops me abruptly and gives me an angry look.

"Hey, look at me," he signs firmly. "I love you no matter what, okay? You're much better than all these idiots in this town," he nods in Tara's direction. "You're the strongest person I know, and I'll always admire you. Never forget that."

I smile slowly.

"I still don't understand how you could sleep with her in high school."

His face contorts into a pained grimace.

"I was drunk!"

Whatever you say, big bro.

Jared

I stare at Hartley's butt in that red skirt, unable to tear my eyes away. She's having tea with Jenna, her mom, and Sawyer, chatting away. It's strange to see my brother in the middle of a group of girls talking, he is so relaxed chatting with them.

I feel a sharp tingling at the back of my neck. Caleb Knight glares at me with a furrowed brow.

"Stop staring at my sister's ass. At least not when I'm around."

"Understood."

He grins and takes a big gulp of beer. I didn't drink because Saw assigned me the role of chauffeur, which we fought out in a tough game of rock-paper-scissors.

"I can't believe Dr. Jacobson is here," Mick sighs. "I still can't believe it."

"I know what you mean. Why did a big-shot doctor decide to come here?" Caleb counters.

"Some doctors want to expand their travels," I explain, afraid he'll get suspicious if I'm too quiet.

"And our little Hartley is one of the lucky few to see him. How did he even know about our little town? Not that it matters, but it's interesting."

"And he's a private doctor. The mystery around his arrival is fascinating," Caleb rubs his jaw, and then he and Mick look at each other as if in silent communion.

I clear my throat as I pour my tea.

When they both turn to me, I know I'm totally screwed. My stomach drops, and I feel the weight of their knowing gazes.

Would Hartley have figured it out if she wasn't so excited?

"Jared! Does my daughter know?"

"I can explain," I put my hands in front of me. "No, she doesn't. I haven't told her yet because I was afraid..."

"She wouldn't go through with it," Caleb nods. "Man... it's going to be hard as hell to hate you after this."

"Glad that was a part of my plan," I snort.

Mick squeezes my shoulder with teary eyes.

"Son, I... I don't know what to say. Do you have any idea how much this means, not only to her but to us? My little girl will finally be able to hear again, and it's all thanks to you."

"And the doctor," I point out.

"You must have paid him a fortune to put my little sister at the top of the list, huh?"

Actually, there is no list. Dr. Jacobson is only here for Hart, but I'd rather not say that part out loud.

"Sorry, I just," Mick shakes his head. "Is it hot in here?"

Damn, even my eyes are burning, but I'm not going to cry in front of them. If I could hold in the tears before, I can keep them in now.

"Yeah, there's definitely something in the air," Caleb wrinkles his nose, but his eyes are suspiciously red.

We stand there, three tall, imposing men, sniffling and lying not only to each other but to ourselves in a way that would make a Broadway director laugh his ass off.

"Hey, what's wrong?" says the woman we are all now keeping a secret from, and I pull her over to me.

"It's just my allergies," Mick sniffs as he signs.

"Oh, you're all three allergic," she looks around in confusion. "I don't want to know what you're talking about," she mumbles, and I kiss her. "Shall we go?"

"Sure, you have a big day on Monday, and my teammates are coming to visit. Thanks for having us over for dinner tonight."

I shake Mick's hand, and he pulls me into a tight bear hug. It's not too surprising, but Caleb does the same.

We walk to the jeep after everyone says goodbye to Hande and Jenna.

"Wow, I've never seen my dad and brother cry in front of my boyfriend before," she shakes her head.

Oh, baby, you'll cry, too, when you find out my secret. I'm just not sure it'll be for joy.

Hartley

The big day has finally come.

When I was a little girl, I thought that when I wrote this in my diary, it would be my wedding day, not a surgery that would hopefully restore my hearing.

Jared helped me move in with him yesterday because he wants to help me while I recover. He thought it would be easier to stay at his place because there is a bathroom connected to the primary bedroom and there is only one bathroom down the hall in my cabin. There is a possibility I may have some nausea the first week after surgery, so not having to run down the hall is probably for the best. Sawyer offered to stay at my cabin so we could have some quiet while I adjust to everything. I put the rest of my clothes in a small bag and take it next door while Jared picks up his friends who arrived today.

I'm nervous about meeting two of his closest friends, but mostly because I have no idea how they'll react to me. Will they like me or treat me differently because I can't hear them?

When I see the driveway, my heart pounds nervously. I watch as a man and a woman get out of the back while another man gets out of the passenger seat. One is dark blond with stubble, while the other looks more like Jared with his dark wavy hair and build. The woman is beautiful as she steps beside her partner. She ties up a section of her light brown shoulder-length hair and begins to fan herself violently. As soon as they're out of sight, I pull myself together and go next door.

I don't know if I'm nervous about the surgery or if I am anxious because they are here.

The door is open when I get there, but I knock anyways because I don't want to disturb anyone. I leave my bag in the living room and go to the kitchen. As I enter, Jared suddenly turns and looks at me with the softest look of pure adoration.

"Hi, Poppy," he leans down and kisses me, not a bit shy.

I can feel the blush creeping up my cheeks, and I peek out from behind him. The men look at me in surprise, and the woman almost melts.

"Hi."

"Hartley, right?" she circles the counter, giving me a gentle hug. "Jared tells me that you can read lips. How do I say my name?" she looks at Jared cluelessly, which makes me laugh.

"That's okay. Jared has already told me about you. Marleen, right?"

"Yes, and that's my husband," she waves at the blond guy with the biggest smile I've ever seen.

"Jason," I nod, reaching out my hand to shake his, he takes my hand and pulls me closer to him, planting two kisses on my cheeks instead.

"Did I do good, babe?" he looks at his wife. "That's what Europeans do, right?"

My boyfriend looks at them in horror, as if he doesn't know who they are.

"You're overdoing it, really."

"Oh, you can never have too much kindness," I wave him off. "You could learn something from them."

Marleen grins and raises her hand for a high-five, and I slap it.

"You're perfect for Jared. You broke his horns."

Jared is pushed aside by the last guest, who must be his best friend from back home, Cage. As he grins broadly, I see that he has dimples on his face like mine.

He pulls me into a bear hug so tight it feels like he might break a rib. He even lifts me up, and Jared's nervous look doesn't break his good mood. When he lets go, he looks at me gratefully, and I feel like this is a very intimate moment. Surprise runs through me when I see him sign.

"Thank you!"

I don't know what he's referring to, but I know when he looks at Jared. He is thanking me for being there for his friend. I don't know why I was so nervous to meet him.

"You learned to sign," Jared states, looking at Cage blankly.

"Just wanted to impress your girl" he winks back. "I only learned three words fast, but I had to tell her."

Cage throws a thousand-watt grin in Jared's direction, who shakes his head and pulls his friend away from me. He runs a hand over my cheek and studies my face for a few moments with a gentle smile.

"Are you okay?" he asks, signing.

"I'm scared," I confess.

"Me too, but it's going to be okay."

"We need to get going," he says, looking slightly down. I nod, and when I turn to say goodbye to his friends, I see them watching us emotionally. Marleen wipes her eyes and shakes her head, covering her eyes.

"I'm sorry, I'm just... so happy to see this."

I suppose they all saw Jared and Meghan's dwindling relationship. I want to prove that I'm better than her, but it appears they already accept me.

"I hope we can talk more soon," I wave.

After we say goodbye, we jump in the car to get to the clinic on time. Jared holds my hand tightly, and I can feel his nervousness. I watch him closely as he lifts my hand to his lips and kisses it. As I replay the events leading up to today in my mind, my heart beats faster and faster. And now here we are. Here's this guy who, despite acting like an idiot when we first met, has fixed up my house, bought me lunch every day, surprised me when I wasn't expecting it, and taken me on this journey I've longed for.

Time seems to fly when we are together. We have come so far since the day we first met, but when his eyes catch mine, I have no doubt about my feelings for him. I've fallen completely in love with this man, and when I hear his voice, I know I'll be lost in him forever.

He turns his whole body towards me before we get out.

"Are you ready?"

No.

"Yes!"

Jared

I pace into the waiting room and take a seat with my friends. Hartley's parents and brother are sitting behind us.

Cage sits beside me, and Marleen and Jason sit across from us. I told them to stay at my chalet as long as they wanted, but they insisted on coming to the hospital with us. They want to offer support, which I'm grateful for, but I know it's not just about me. Hartley stole their hearts in two minutes by looking at me in a way Meghan never did.

They wheeled her into surgery about ten minutes ago, and I've been a restless savage ever since.

"It's gonna be okay, buddy. Can I get you some coffee?" Jason stands up.

"Thanks," I smile at him. "I'll take an espresso, please. No, make it an Americano. Iced. Maybe with a little cinnamon?"

"Yeah. Okay. Do you guys want anything?" he turns to the others.

"A nonfat latte, thinly topped with whipped cream and chocolate drizzle," Marleen answers quietly.

"I'll have a cappuccino," Cage says. "Low-fat milk with agave syrup, about a finger."

"Okay, I'm just asking out of fucking politeness. How do you expect me to remember all that?"

Then he walks out, leaving us there.

"Hey," Marleen nods in my direction. "That girl is perfect for you. I can't wait to get to know her better."

"Careful, looks can be deceiving," I smile. "She's naughty, and sometimes she can be terrifying."

"I like her even more now."

"What did you say to her before they wheeled her back?" I turn to Cage.

"That's between us," he shrugs. "But I've never seen you so happy. "Looking at you now, compared to when you left Montreal, it's like night and day," he reflects. "Back then, I wasn't sure if you'd ever break free from that rut, no matter how much you fought. It felt like you'd given up on finding the silver lining in life, you know?"

"It wasn't necessarily about Meghan," I mumble.

"No, brother, it was about all the women you were disappointed in. You picked wrong; you looked in the wrong place."

"Or," Marleen stretches the word and leans forward on her knees. "You subconsciously settled for superficial relationships because you feared something more serious."

"Initially, maybe, but with Meghan, I was genuinely committed. I just misread the situation. That's when I realized how great it would be to meet a genuinely good woman and how challenging it can be in a world where people often gravitate towards you for your wealth and status," I explain. "Jason got lucky."

"Oh, Jared... I knew you'd get lucky one day, and look, you did," she smiles. "Cage isn't a hopeless case either, once he finally gets out of the bear's den."

Cage has been lying low for ages. He's a bit of a lone wolf, always off on his own. And I don't blame him for being cautious around women, given his past. It's also because of his kid, and I know the kid is now with his sister. His mini version loves it there.

My friend leans his head back against the wall, lost in thought. I want to talk to him because I've been feeling sidelined since I got here a few weeks back. We've both had our plates full, but I've always made time for him. Yet, he hasn't really taken me up on it, and that's bugging me. I don't want him keeping all his shit bottled up, especially since I'm guilty of doing that too. Marleen seems to sense something's up as she slowly gets up from her chair.

"I'm going to find Jason. Are you okay?"

"Sure, go ahead," I nod, and she walks away. "Coach told me you're quitting. What the hell happened?"

"You already know Jason got picked up by Vancouver." I nod.

"Two teams came for me," he sighs. "Jared, he sold me to the Lion Knights," he looks at me with a tired expression. I stare at him in shock as I process what I've just heard.

"We hate that team."

"I know."

"You hate it the most."

"And I haven't accepted it. I'm leaving the NHL."

"Cage!"

"Listen, you should understand. I'm slow, I'm getting slower, and I'm turning thirty. How much time do I have? Five years? Ten at best? But in my case, that's out of the question. I am not an Ovechkin or a Sidney Crosby. Everybody knows that, even me. Do you know what everyone was talking about after you left? What will happen to me without you now that the duo is broken up? I was the best with you. You were the best to play with, and I didn't even play the last few games; I was always on the bench. So I'm sorry, I don't want to spend the last years of my career just watching what happens. I'd rather be an active part of it."

Hell, how could I not understand? If there was anyone who had suffered many injuries in their career besides me, it was him. He wasn't even sure if he could return to the ice after his last one, but he did it anyway for his own sake.

Cage rubs his dark stubble and grins at me.

"We were good, though. We really tore up the ice."

"Good times," I nod. "Sorry. If you stay, Coach might offer you a job. I turned him down, but I think you'd like it."

"We'll see. Right now, I just want to enjoy the rest of the season and see what happens."

"There's always your teaching degree. If you need help, I could talk to my parents."

"The change of environment worked for you. I may do the same."

"Then you could come here. There's always my spare room," I wink. "We could coach a damn high school team together," I suggest, and he looks at me in horror.

"Yeah? Teenage kids, I couldn't handle that. But thanks for the offer, I'll pass."

"Then why the hell did you choose a career in teaching?"

He laughs out loud. Shit, I missed that sound.

"Now, let's worry about your girlfriend. Jason and Marleen leave in a few days, but I'll stay for a week or two. We'll have time to talk things through."

"Thanks for being here," I squeeze his shoulder.

"I imagine you'll need some help while she recovers, so I offer my wonderful services wholeheartedly," he looks at me smugly.

"If you make a move on my girl, I'll kill you."

"I would never do that!"

Someone gasps and runs into the waiting room. Jenna stops with a tired, worn look on her face, clutching a large coffee cup. She flicks her dark curls out of her face and lets out a hard breath.

"I tried to be here sooner but got stuck in traffic."

"Hartley's already inside; we're waiting. Have a seat," I point to the chair. She says hello to Hartley's parents before sitting down next to me.

Cage looks over at her appreciatively, and for a moment, his gaze lingers on her butt. I slap him on the back of the head, and he glares at me.

"Jenna, this is my best friend, Cage."

She reaches over and shakes his hand.

"Nice to meet you. I thought Danny was your best friend."

"Yes, please explain it to me," Cage gives me a cheeky look, and I want to slap him again.

"Well... here, Danny is my best friend. And Cage is at home," I explain.

"And if I move here?"

"Then you'll have to challenge Danny to a duel, and I'll be the judge."

"Me too!" Jenna raises her hand. Cage is still staring at her, and he slowly smiles at the fact that she's completely embarrassed by him and continues to look away nervously.

Jenna looks back at my friend with a piercing stare, who continues to watch her absentmindedly.

That's cool. If they get along so well, they might be married by the time Hartley gets out of surgery.

"Behave," I hiss at Cage. "She's Hart's best friend."

"But she looks like she wants to kick me in the balls."

"Because you're undressing her with your eyes."

Cage snorts, Jenna sighs, and I want to run away.

Marleen and Jason finally come back, four coffees in hand. My eyes are already throbbing from lack of caffeine, so I grab the cup held out like a bloodhound. I introduce them to Jenna, who immediately finds common ground with Marleen.

"Instant coffee, cold water," he gestures towards the cup before handing one to Cage. "Coffee with milk. Enjoy."

I peer into the cup, noticing strange brown specks floating on top. "What's that?"

"I added a sprinkle of cinnamon for you," he replies, taking a seat. "Did you know there's only a tiny cafeteria around here? I had to whip these up myself because the lady nearly kicked me out when I placed our order."

Ah, that explains it. I scoop the scattered cinnamon pieces onto the cup's rim before pouring in the watery coffee. Now, that's a proper Americano.

"I think this milk is out of date," Cage leans over to me.

"That's why you should drink black coffee in every strange place. It's hard to go wrong."

"Hey, did you know there's an artisanal coffee shop next door?" Jenna sips her drink smugly, and Jason stares at her blankly. "But... I'm sure the homemade version is pretty good, too," she clears her throat.

Caleb joins our group and all kinds of questions and stories follow. The most embarrassing story is Jenna's, which Marleen gets a kick out of. It's incredible how she can make friends so quickly, just like Hartley.

Hartley

The street is covered in snow, and the cars and trees are hidden from view by the raging storm. I rub my eyes, feeling disoriented, like I've been caught off guard. I fought tooth and nail for us, but now it all feels like it was for nothing. Tears mix with the cold as I try to turn up the heat in the car, but I just can't shake off the chill. It's like my tears are turning to ice against my skin. Then, everything suddenly goes quiet, and this weird tingling sensation washes over me. I can't see the road anymore; maybe I should just pull over. But then I lose control of the wheel. I feel myself spinning, everything whirling out of focus. There's a wall coming at me fast, and then bam! My head hits something hard, and it's lights out.

Then, I wake up.

Jared

At ten o'clock sharp, the doctor emerges from the operating room and joins us in the waiting area. Despite his weariness, his eyes shine with relief, assuring us everything went smoothly.

"Everything went well," he nods. "She's still sleeping. As soon as she wakes, you can go in and see her. But not at the same time. One person," he points at me.

I look at Jenna and Hartley's family, trying to work out how we should go about this.

"I..."

"No, Jared! I want you to go in first. I know that's what Hartley wants. We've got time," Hande says quickly.

Am I being selfish by wanting her to hear my voice first? But she's Hartley's mom. Still, when I look into her eyes, it's as if she's silently telling me that she really wants this, and if it's what Hart really wants, I want to give it to her.

"Thanks," I mutter, catching the depth of her emotion. Tears sting my eyes as I meet her gaze. She pulls me into a hug, and though I'm a bit uncertain, I hug her back, knowing she needs this as much as I do.

Jenna grabs me for another hug before I can sit back down. I can feel her unspoken words of gratitude in her embrace. She reminds me of Cage, who cares for me just as deeply. They both hide their own struggles to support others until it all spills out. I never realized how tough it was for him because he never let on. Was Hartley the same, just too strong to show her pain?

Time drags by painfully slow until Hartley finally wakes up, and the doctor clears her for visitors. When the nurse calls us over, I jump, returning to the moment.

"Can I see her?" I ask hastily, and the middle-aged woman nods with a smile.

"Follow me. She's still a bit groggy from being placed under anesthesia. She was quite scared when she woke and cried quite a bit," she says with a sad but kind look. "She'll be very happy to see you, I'm sure."

I'm shaking, my chest is pounding, and my palms are clammy. My heart is beating so fast. By the time we reach Hartley's door, I feel like I'm going to faint.

It's time.

Hartley

I'm a little woozy from the sedation, and my body is still tingling with numbness. It's like my senses have been turned down for a while and then turned up to the max. I let out a shaky sigh, and I... hear it.

The sound of the monitor and the sounds coming from outside. I hear them.

The sounds make my head pound, and I grind my teeth in discomfort. I hear it.

The click and the soft creak of the door opening. I hear that, too.

My eyes sting, already swollen from a good cry, as I wake up to the doctor looking at me. I was unable to hear what he was saying, and for a moment, I was afraid; what if my brain could not put the words together between the sounds?

Jared stuck his head in and entered the room. He looked so nervous I almost laughed. He carefully closes the door with a soft click.

I clench my jaw, afraid I'll cry before he speaks.

He walks over to the bed and pulls out a chair. He falls into it as he reaches for my hand.

"Hi, baby," he says in a low, hoarse voice, and I feel my heart sink into my stomach.

"Hi," I sob softly, tears flooding my eyes again. "I can hear your voice," I sniffle. "I-I can really hear you."

"Fuck, Hart," he groans as he pulls my hand to his mouth.

A pleasant, deep sound comes from his throat like the most beautiful bass being played. I may have dreamed it to be much deeper, but the reality is even better than I could have imagined.

"Speak some more," I ask quietly.

"Your cheeks are the same poppy-red now as when I first kissed you," he smiles, and I see his eyes darken.

"Because I cried like a baby," I laugh softly, having to control myself not to sign my words. It helps that he squeezes my hand as if he never wants to let go.

Jared watches me with a penetrating gaze, and I am, perhaps, completely embarrassed to be in front of him for the first time. It's like seeing and getting to know him all over again. He gets up and sits cautiously on the edge of my bed, his eyes tracing the bandage on my head. As he leans down to me, the scent of winter, pine, and sandalwood creeps into my nostrils.

"Hi," he greets me again.

"Hi," I laugh softly as his nose touches mine. "Tell me more," I ask again.

"You're so beautiful," he strokes my tired face. "I can't wait to get home and finally be alone with you. I won't let anyone interrupt us."

"Don't bet on it," I snort.

I know that Danny and Maggie plan to visit us at the cabin tomorrow. And Sawyer is having a hard time being alone. Maybe his friends will also stop by. They rented one of the cabins across the lake for a few days.

"Your eyes are like green leaves in a field of poppies. So alive," he kisses me tenderly.

"Go on," I sigh.

His soft voice is like a melody.

"Did you know that when we met, I wanted to stick my fingers in those two deep dimples on your cheeks?"

"Jared," I laugh.

"Your upper lip forms the perfect shape of a heart. I think it's called a Cupid's Bow."

"More," I huff. His eyes soften, but there's a hint of mischief in them.

His lips trace my jawline, and the heat in my chest spreads.

"I'm crazy about you."

"More..."

"I fantasize about you always; there's so much I want to do to you."

"More," I laugh because I think I'll never get enough of his voice. He tilts his forehead to mine and sighs.

"I hope you know you turned my world upside down, and I wouldn't change it for the world."

He's not alone. Before him, my life was like still water, calm and quiet. But even though I couldn't hear him, he stirred up those waters, bringing a whole new energy and excitement into my life.

"I want to take this hospital gown off of you and slide my hand..."

"God!"

Someone knocks on the door as Jared straightens.

Dr. Jacobson enters the room with the nurse behind him, who has visited me a few times.

I'm asked a couple of questions, and as I answer, Jared takes my hand in his, tracing reassuring circles on my wrist.

"I'll oversee your recovery for the rest of the week, and then my partner will take over. He'll remove the bandages in two weeks."

We discuss how often and when I'll have to come back. Jared listens intently. I will be given an antibiotic medication to take for the next week and earplugs to use if I need a break from the sound.

"What do I do if she can't stay on her butt and wants to go back to work?"

I feel like a little kid in trouble.

"I'm not sure I want to go back to Moonlight with a bandage on my head," I mutter. "But I insist on working from home."

"See? That's what I'm talking about," he points at me.

"Some people return to work after about a week, depending on how they are feeling. If you feel up to it, there's nothing wrong with working from home."

I give Jared a satisfied smile.

"I understand, thank you. She will be able to go home tomorrow morning, right?"

"That's right. I'll prescribe the extra antibiotics."

The doctor leaves us alone, and I lean back wearily. I don't even realize I'm drifting off to sleep until Jared's soft voice and gentle strokes on my arm begin to soothe the tension that's been building in my head for what feels like forever.

Jared

I think the hospital staff is ready for me to leave. Having spent the night in an uncomfortable chair in Hart's room, I'd jump up as soon as they came in to check on her and watch their every move like I was her guard dog. I am sure I looked like a half-zombie and scared a few patients when I went looking for coffee at 5 a.m.

When Hartley was finally discharged at eight o'clock, I made a dash to catch the doctor outside the ward in time.

"Dr. Jacobson," I called after him. "I wanted to thank you."

He shakes my hand in surprise.

"It was my pleasure, son. Your timing was perfect, and since I'm heading to Vancouver anyhow, changing my flight wasn't much trouble. But I'm curious," he says, giving me a puzzled look. "Why specifically reach out to me for this? Any doctor could've handled the procedure."

"I wanted the best," I assert firmly. "Only the best, nothing less."

He gazes into my eyes momentarily as if trying to find something, then nods and walks away. Well, I suppose that went smoothly.

*

"Carefully," I lead Hartley into the house, balancing her bag in one hand.

"Jared, I can walk just fine; my head is bandaged, not my body."

"Yeah, but you might get dizzy or have a headache, and I don't want you to fall over."

Hartley put on the earplugs on the way back to the cabin so the sound of the horns and cars wouldn't hurt her ears. I tried not to speak loudly, even though I wanted to say everything I felt and thought.

As we step into the kitchen, Danny and Maggie are already there, ready with lunch. I nearly have to intervene to stop them from squeezing Hart too tightly, mindful of Hart's condition. Alright, I'll admit it—I'm a bit of an overprotective bastard, but I won't let anything happen to my girl.

Lucretia appears out of nowhere and jumps into Danny's lap.

"I can't believe you've barely spent time with that cat, and she's already your best friend."

Danny just shrugs, wearing a smitten grin, while he gives the cat some ear scratches.

"I'm so happy for you," Maggie whispers, taking Hart's hand.

"We could hardly contain ourselves. I stopped by the hospital last night to bring Jared a change of clothes. Who knows how long it's been since he's had a shower," Danny says quietly.

Hartley pulls out the earplugs.

"What?"

"I said quietly, not a whisper," I sigh.

"Oh, okay, I'll turn up my volume," Maggie winks. "I brought cinnamon rolls and made Milanese pork ribs for lunch. I hope that sounds okay."

"And if it's not?" I ask.

"You can starve," she chides.

"Maggie's Milanese pork chops are world champion," Danny winks as he finishes setting the table.

"I'm starving," Hartley groans. I get her settled in a chair at the table before preparing a plate of food for her. I scoop out a large portion of the noodles and pile the crispy, sizzling meat on top. She watches with bulging eyes.

"Is this enough food? I want you to eat well."

Before she has a chance to respond, the door slams shut loudly. Sawyer rushes excitedly into the kitchen, grabbing Hart from behind, but he's careful not to squeeze too hard. She lets out a squeak of surprise but quickly relaxes, casting a suspicious glance over her shoulder.

"I brought you some flowers," Sawyer says quietly, presenting a bouquet of poppies. It's clear he just plucked them from the ground, as bits of mud still fall from the roots.

"Oh, wow, thank you! Is this my welcome home gift?"

My brother stands there as if he's done something wrong, looking around the kitchen with a clenched jaw.

"It's more like an apology."

"Why?"

Saw sighs heavily and steps back.

"I added some design changes to your plan while you were gone," he mumbles and then runs off. I look after him, stunned.

"What?" Hartley blurts out angrily, slowly getting to her feet. "Sawyer!"

I hear the idiot lock the bathroom door behind him. Hart chases after him, and I listen to the unfolding events with a sense of satisfaction.

"Sawyer! Come out now!"

"No!" I can hear his muffled voice all the way over here.

"Open the door!"

"No!"

"I see your brother and girlfriend are getting along," Danny grins.

"They love each other; they just don't know it yet," I smile.

"So, are your friends from Montreal here?" he asks.

"Yes, and I hope you and Cage keep it down."

They met two years ago when Cage came with me to visit my grandmother. They decided to settle the score with a doughnut-eating challenge at the summer festival, each fighting to be crowned "my best friend." They both ended up throwing up in the bushes, and I had to drive them home covered in vomit. They will both always be my best friends, but I did enjoy watching them fight like schoolboys.

"I'm going to keep it cool, but just a heads up, there's a beer-drinking contest at the festival."

"Danny," Maggie sighs. "Instead of continuing this unnecessary battle you and Cage can't seem to shake, you should ask Jared how it felt to talk to Hartley for the first time when she woke up," she pleads, and I push hard into my hair. It's long now and could use a trim.

"I can't put it into words... The look on her face when she first heard me was indescribable."

Even now, there are moments when she glances at me as if she's seeing me for the first time, and it's adorable how she blushes and seems flustered by the sound of my voice.

I'll speak to her all night if she asks, just to please her. I can't wait to pleasure her in other ways when she feels up to it as well. Just thinking about her makes my cock throb.

"I've never seen you in love before," she rests her chin on her hand.

"I haven't..." I start but don't finish. Arguing would be useless because they're right. My heart was already Hartley's when I reached out to Coach for help, perhaps even before that, when I dashed over to her house, green with jealousy, and gave her a piece of my mind about her brother.

"Yeah, I know what I am talking about," Maggie laughs.

Hartley

I think Jared goes a bit overboard with his worrying, but his sweetness just melts my heart. He's been constantly asking me what I need these past few days, and many times, he's done things he thought I needed without even asking. He's cooked my favorite meals, and when he's been stuck, he's either ordered takeout or enlisted Maggie's help. He's given me shoulder massages, and whenever I've drifted off on the couch, I've always woken up wrapped up like a burrito, even when it's been boiling outside.

I've never been with someone as considerate as Jared, and every time I realize it, I can't help but involuntarily compare him to Brody. The moment the comparison crosses my mind, my stomach tightens. I've never had dreams about the accident, which should probably be a relief.

As I sit alone in the cabin in the afternoon, surrounded by the clock's ticking, birds chirping, and the gentle lapping of lake water, a sense of unease washes over me. Lucretia and Cocoa keep me company. Jared brought the baby goat to me because he knew how much I missed him, and he said Cocoa hadn't been the same since I left. So now I have a narcissistic cat curled up on one side of me and a homeless baby goat on the other. The little guy even has a tag with his name on it.

Jared headed over to the Moonlight earlier this morning to map out the next week and a half because he wants to stay at the cabin with me. It'll be comforting to have someone by my side, helping me keep my mind off the overwhelming sensation of being able to hear every little thing again.

Someone knocks on the door. I turn around, about to get up to answer the door when I see Eric stepping into the house. He's holding a box of cookies, and I recognize my mom's store logo. Did he really buy sweets from her when my mom would've sent them to him for free? It's heartwarming to see him supporting the family business.

"Hi, beautiful."

Oh my God... This is the first time I've ever heard it. I've pictured his voice in my head so many times over the past two years; it's like I've heard it before. He has a slightly higher, raspier voice than Jared. Similar to Sawyer.

"Nice bandage," he points at my head.

"Just keeping up with the latest fashion trends."

He sits down next to me, causing Lucretia to run away, and plants a kiss on my cheek. He looks confused at the goat on my other side, whose ears I'm scratching, but doesn't mention it.

"I brought you some of your mom's goodies. This honey and nut cake is delicious," he sighs. "I got it for myself, but I hope you like it."

"Like doesn't even begin to describe how I feel about Marlenka."

"I brought you some new gossip as well. I went to the town meeting. For now, you're excused from what you've been running from for weeks, but as soon as you're better, you'll have to face the town on the nude bathing issue."

"Oh no," I groan.

"McRoyal is on a rampage because he thinks Jared's NHL friends will stay too long. He's afraid the crazy fans will start invading our town and have no respect for the traditions or people here."

"Bob's getting a little carried away."

"He also said he wishes you a speedy recovery."

"He can be nice sometimes," I sigh.

"And Jenna has been trying to stay away from a hockey player who apparently has his eyes set on her. I don't get how someone can feel stalked by just a glance, but I think it's some kind of internal phobia she has about athletes."

"Cage was definitely staring at her, according to Jared."

"As soon as you recover, we'll assess the situation. You seem a little off. Are you okay? Are you having sex?"

"I got my head cut into," I exaggerate, slightly irritated. "Of course, I'm a little off."

"So you're not having sex," he points out. "Is Jared worried about hurting you? You said he likes it rough."

"Eric," I cover my face for a moment, but he just raises an eyebrow questioningly. "He won't touch me," I blurt out. "I get that he's scared, but... ever since we've been sleeping together, he's been staying as far away from me as he can on the bed because he's 'afraid he'll squeeze my head.'"

"This guy is adorable," he laughs, trying not to be too loud. I don't tell him he doesn't have to sign anymore, but a part of me finds it comforting.

"I was thinking of jumping on him and ordering him to touch me."

"Order him?"

"Why is he the only one in charge?" I grin. "Maybe he would like it if I took control."

"Get it, girl," he winks, then stands from the couch. "So what now? Shall we make some coffee and inhale this box of delicious carbs?"

"Hell, yes!"

Jared

A sense of Déjà vu hits me as my brother spins in my office chair. At the same time, I type up my vacation notice and send out a few emails letting people know they can reach me online for the next week or at the chalet.

Sawyer's fingers tap rhythmically on the chair's elbow rest; then, he turns to face me.

"I bankrupt my company."

I immediately stop typing and stare at him.

"We lost a lot of money, the company went bankrupt, and Grandma knew about it. I didn't actually come to visit because I lost my creativity. I came because I was broke. All I have left is a small savings account that is nearly gone, too. So there you go, that's why I am here."

"Sawyer... Why didn't you tell me you were in trouble?"

"That's why I came to you first. Grandma encouraged me, and I knew if there was anyone I could run to, it was you. I love Mom, Dad, and Brianna, but I didn't want to feel like I needed to be coddled or given any sympathy. I didn't want to go home. Being here is my only job now, and I trust you the most. I need a job, brother, badly. So... please hire me. I'll interview if I have to, submit my portfolio, do a mock interview."

"I'll discuss it with management," I nod. "Fuck, I didn't see this coming. Everything was going so well."

"Yeah, except for my judgment when I left everything to my investor who screwed me after three years and walked away with not only my clients but the money," he smiles. "Fuck you!"

"Did something happen between the two of you?"

"Does it matter that I slept with his fiancee?"

"What the fuck, Saw!"

"I didn't know!" he shouts. "I'm sorry, but the woman at the bar didn't mention anything about being my investor's fiancée. She wasn't even wearing her damn ring. It's like she was deliberately trying to set me up, or who knows; maybe he sent her to me so he'd have an excuse to ruin me."

"I doubt someone would willingly let their fiancee sleep with another man," I mutter. "Thanks for telling me, bro. I will help you as much as I can. At least now we know what we're dealing with."

"I thought I'd talk to Kelly and see if she can use her connections to look into it."

"Good idea," I sigh. "Now I should get going. I miss my girl."

"It's nice to have someone to come home to, isn't it," he sighs theatrically.

"You know you can always come over between five and eight in the evening."

I've set strict rules so he doesn't barge in at the wrong time.

"I doubt you'd let me in a threesome, so I'd rather not bother," he shudders, and damn it, that makes me shudder. Why does he have to say shit like that?

*

I swing by the store to pick up my surprise before heading home. I place Hartley's gift in the back seat, hoping she'll like it. I even splurged on a cute little poppy-printed case for it, getting one of the painters at the Moonlight to customize it for me.

Before I enter the house, I lean the present against the door and head inside to find Hartley. She's curled up on the couch, fast asleep. I smile and approach her quietly. There's a book resting on her chest, and I notice a new blog post on the laptop screen. As I draw closer, something suddenly catches my eye at the bottom of the screen, causing me to pause.

This is a list... *Things I am Thankful For.*

- *Sounds and melodies*
- *Wonderful friends*

- *Bizarre but fantastic families*
- *and Jared Zykov*

"Hey," Hart says sleepily, slowly opening her eyes.
"Hey. You fell asleep."
"I'm exhausted and in a food coma because of Eric," she groans as she stands up, and I help her up. "Are you okay?"
"More than okay, Poppy," I whisper. "You know I'm proud of you, right?"
"Why is that?"
"For everything," I kiss her softly and she sighs. "Hey, I brought you something."
"Oh, a present. I like the sound of that," her eyes light up.
"I wanted to ask you, what happened to that guitar you played in the videos?"
"In my mom's attic," she looks at me questioningly. "Why?"
I walk back to the door and carry the new guitar in its case into the living room. Hartley's eyes widen.
"I don't believe it!"
"Open it," I hand it to her. She throws herself at it like a little kid, which makes me laugh.
Shuddering, she pulls out the acoustic guitar and puts it on her lap. Then she does something I didn't expect and sniffs the guitar. She even wrinkles her nose.
Shuddering, she pulls out the acoustic guitar and sets it on her lap. Then, to my surprise, she leans in and takes a deep breath, her expression shifting with curiosity.
"It smells like fresh pine and sunshine. Oh, Jared, thank you."
Setting the guitar down, she practically leaps into my arms, and I bury my face in her neck, relishing her warmth. Is she the only one who can sense it? I wonder.
"You're welcome, Poppy. Go ahead, try it out. I know you want to."

She excitedly takes the guitar back and starts strumming. I asked the salesman to tune it for me so she could play it immediately.

"I'm out of practice," she mumbles as she plays quietly. "I never thought I would be able to play guitar again. I'm so happy."

I inhale sharply, feeling my head swim and my vision blur. The weight of the emails and her emotional response to the music becomes overwhelming. The tears of joy in her eyes wrench at my heart, and I know I can't keep suppressing what I've been holding inside for weeks.

"I'll be right back," I manage to choke out.

Hurrying onto the porch, I collapse into one of the chairs. And then it hits me like a tidal wave. I burst into tears, soft sobs escaping me as I grip my hair tightly and bury my face in my hands.

In that moment, everything I've suspected becomes unmistakably clear. I'm completely in love with this woman. I've given her what she desired most, and now I'm ready to give her the world and pluck the stars from the sky if it means bringing her happiness.

*

"Gosh!" I blurt out suddenly, immediately wincing as I feel a twinge in my stiff neck.

Lucretia scratches my arm and gives me a nervous look, which is unusual for her. Damn, I must have dozed off on the porch.

"What's the matter, girl?" I ask, looking at her.

"Meow!"

And then I leap to my feet as she bolts off the porch. Peering through the open door, I see that Hart has fallen asleep on the couch. I rush after Lucretia, following her to Cocoa's little shed. But what I find there is unexpected: the baby goat staggering towards me. And then... he collapses.

Jared gently rouses me from my sleep, his face etched with concern as he cradles Cocoa in his arms.

"There's something wrong with Cocoa. I need to rush him to the vet," he explains urgently.

"I'm coming with you."

I hastily throw on my sweater and join Jared as we head to the Jeep. I take Cocoa from him, allowing him to focus on driving. The poor goat appears to be drifting in and out of consciousness, occasionally stirring only to collapse again, soiling himself.

As we wait, doubt creeps in, making me wonder if we've accidentally caused Cocoa harm. I rack my brain, retracing our steps over the past few hours, but I can't remember anything unusual in his diet.

A nurse takes Cocoa from us, ushering us to the waiting room while she tends to him. Jared sighs wearily, wrapping an arm around me.

"I've been neglecting him lately," he admits, his voice tinged with guilt. "Ever since we finished the fence, I haven't paid much attention to him. What if he is not okay? You mentioned his panic attacks. I won't forgive myself if I'm the reason he's in trouble."

"Jared, he's going to be fine," I soothe, trying to ease his worries. "I texted Maggie, who's experienced with goats. It could be a bacterial infection or a virus. They'll give him some medicine, and he'll be okay."

We settle into our seats, anxiously awaiting news. Finally, the doctor emerges, and we stand up eagerly.

"Cocoa's parents?" he inquires, and we approach him quickly. "Everything's fine; he just picked up a minor virus. You can come in, and I'll brief you on what you need to do and provide you with some medication."

Relief floods over me as Jared squeezes my hand. I didn't know it was possible, but I'm even more enamored with him now. What guy would rush a goat to the hospital at night because he's worried he may have caused it harm?

*

We enter a refurbished wooden shed, and I'm in awe of Jared's work. I hadn't yet had the chance to see it amidst everything else going on. Inside, there are cozy wool blankets, a waterer, and a feeder laid out. Under different circumstances, I might consider it a bit extravagant, but not now. We wrap Cocoa in one of the blankets and settle beside him.

"Would it be alright if I stay with him tonight?" Jared asks softly. "I just want to make sure he's okay."

"Of course," I insist, covering my legs as I sit beside the goat. "I'm staying too."

"Baby..."

"I'm staying!" I assert, gripping his hand firmly. He looks at me with a soft smile before reclining back, gently petting Cocoa. Lucretia strolls in, curling up between us and showing her concern by nuzzling Cocoa.

It's certainly an unusual scene, with various scents filling the air. Yet, there's a comforting warmth and a feeling of being right where we belong as we snuggle with these animals we've grown attached to over the summer. Despite the unconventional setting, there's a sense of happiness in the presence of goat poop and the distinct scent of a cat that I've never felt before.

It's like our own little family.

Jared

I am woken up in the morning by something wet and warm on my face. Opening my eyes, I'm met with Cocoa's giant blue eyes and his toothy grin as he continues to lick my face.

"Cocoa, are you alright?" I ask, sitting up and pulling the goat into a tight hug, relieved to see him awake. Lucretia is no longer with us, but her presence is still evident on the blanket beside Hartley.

Hartley slowly opens her eyes, looking sleepily at Cocoa. She sits up so quickly that I worry she might have hurt herself. There's a bit of dried drool on the corner of her mouth, which she quickly wipes away. Despite her disheveled appearance, she's still the most beautiful girl I've ever seen. We spent the night out here together, along with a goat and a cat that I still can't quite understand.

"Hey, little buddy," Hartley says, reaching out to pet Cocoa, who nuzzles against her.

She presses Cocoa's nose into her palm and strokes him affectionately. Then, as if we're no longer interesting, Cocoa turns away and bounds out of the shed like nothing happened.

"Well, it looks like everything's back to normal," I say, leaning back.

Hartley chuckles softly. "We stink."

"And I was thinking of kissing you."

"After Cocoa licked your face, I'd rather take a shower," she replies, and I can't help but smile.

"Yeah, let's definitely take a shower," I suggest, looking over at her. "Together."

A blush spreads across her cheeks, but I can see the excitement in her eyes. She never could hide it from me.

Despite feeling like a total mess, Hartley's thoughts don't stop us from enjoying each other's company. Still, I can't shake the concern that if we don't shower soon, our friends might pass out from the smell.

Hartley

"And then they were caught on camera drunkenly embracing like lovers," laughs Marleen as she takes a sip of the cider Jenna sent.

They even gave us a special strawberry wine, which I only sipped a little of since I'm on antibiotics and didn't want to risk passing out. My mom would scold me for that. I'm pretty tired after last night, but luckily, Cocoa is alive and well, and so is Jared.

Jason and Marleen came over to our house before heading back to Vancouver, wanting to get to know me a little better. Marleen was doing everything she could to make the boys uncomfortable.

"Come on, the fans loved it," laughs Jared.

"Yeah, I was really jealous," Marleen says, placing her hand on her chest, pretending she is upset. When the boys leave the kitchen, and it's just the two of us, I see an inscrutable smile on her face.

"You know, I've never seen him so happy," she says.

"I don't know what it was like before," I confess. "But he told me a few things."

"Listen, I don't blame anyone for their past. Jared just had a habit of making bad choices."

"Who doesn't make bad choices?"

"All I'm saying is that Meghan didn't deserve him, and Jared realized that too late. I don't think losing Meghan hurt him; it was realizing he made the wrong choice. But now, I believe he's made the best decision possible."

"Where are you going with this?" I ask.

Marleen leans closer to me.

"I don't want to rob Jared of the opportunity to tell you himself, but I've never seen him like this with anyone else. He clearly has fallen so hard for you a tow truck couldn't pull him out," she laughs. "And I'm grateful for that. You know, you're the kind of girl I always pictured him with."

"I was afraid you wouldn't like me."

"Are you out of your mind? You're sweet, funny, and have a tongue sharp enough to toot your own horn when you need to. You're perfect for him. If I were a guy, I'd be all over you," she grins, which I return.

"For what it's worth, I'd be all over you, too, even as a girl."

Marleen winks and raises her glass to me. Then, the boys return.

"Did I hear you hit on my girl, Marleen?" Jared puts his arm around my shoulder.

"I knew you'd get bored. I thought it would only come up after Vancouver, but I was wrong," Jason sighs. "I'm not surprised. Hartley's perfect. Everybody loves her."

"I hope you meant that as a compliment..."

As we eat, we continue our casual conversation, and the wine slowly runs out. It's refreshing to get a glimpse into Jared's life in the NHL, and Marleen and Jason are wonderful. I can't wait to hear more stories about Jared from Cage.

When they say their goodbyes to return to their cabin early, because they have to fly back early in the morning, Marleen pulls me in for a big hug.

"I gave you my number, so you can reach me anytime. And I'll send you the compromising pictures like I promised," she winks.

He growls as he pushes her around like a toddler.

Jared wraps his arms around me from behind after closing the door, resting his chin on my shoulder.

"What pictures?" he asks suspiciously. He looks so alarmed that I have to bite my lip to keep from laughing.

"Oh, that's just for us girls."

He lets go of my hand and pulls me into the kitchen, where dishes and wine glasses are stacked on top of each other.

"Question. Do we clean up now and go to bed late, or do we wait until the morning?"

"I vote now."

"You know what? Let's listen to some music."

"God, there are so many albums on my list," I sigh, rolling up the sleeves of my sweater.

As we tidy up and put away the leftovers, Taylor Swift's rendition of last year's "Speak Now" album starts playing. It's incredible how she continues to revolutionize the music industry with her songs.

I don't know what's more surprising; Jared's cleaning up or the fact that he has every album on my list. I have no idea where he found them.

"I saw your *Things I am Thankful For* list," he says quietly. "I didn't mean to, I swear. I was going to lock your computer, but it just popped up, and I was..."

"Oh…"

"I know. I'm sorry."

"It's all right. I was honest when I wrote the list."

"This means a lot to me, Poppy. I know your ex hurt you, but I don't want to."

I know...

I don't say it out loud, but I hope he doesn't think my ex means anything to me beyond being a former friend who I once cared about despite everything. Then I remember that he has his own demons to face with Meghan. There's a boogeyman hanging over both of us, and it's up to us whether we let it control us. Personally, I refuse to. So, I'm going to use a bit of superficiality to try to snap him out of his reverie.

"You're so much hotter, by the way," I throw out, tapping him playfully on his ass.

Jared pulls his mouth into a big, dimpled grin.

"Baby, I hope you don't think I'm jealous or worried that you're still attached to your ex. I'm really enjoying this connection we have. Keep it up," he says with a wave, and I roll my eyes. "You're way hotter than my ex."

"Is that all..."

Jared laughs heartily, and I melt at the sound of his voice. He keeps finding new ways to embarrass me and warm my heart, and I'm completely under his spell.

I clear my throat.

"Are my tits bigger than hers, at least?"

"Jesus, Poppy," he laughs. "You have nice tits. Let's just say I'm grateful they're real."

"Ouch... I mean, what's it like to hold silicone?" The question slips out of my mouth, and he looks up at me slowly as he puts the last plate in the dishwasher. "I'm genuinely curious."

"It's... unnatural," he says, gesturing as if holding something. "I can't really explain it. Not bad, just… different."

"I used to want to get them," I admit with a strained smile. "But as I got older, I gave up on the idea."

"Please, don't even joke about it. I love your boobs."

"And I love your ass. You have a beautiful ass, Jared Zykov."

"You're in a naughty mood tonight," he looks at me incredulously.

When we're finished, he changes the music. I want to yell at him to let me choose the album, but my shoulders slump as the familiar tune begins to play, one I've known for so long and filled with old memories.

"Dance with me," he offers his hand.

"We danced to this at the ball." I can remember feeling the vibrations of the melody through the ballroom.

"When you had too many drinks, and I had to help get you home? Oh, yes, I remember," he pulls me towards him.

He wraps one arm around my waist, pulling me into his embrace. He lifts my hand to his lips, placing a soft kiss on the inside of my wrist. He starts to gently sway our bodies to the melody as the music plays. I feel his every heartbeat as I snuggle against him, moving slowly in time with the rhythm.

"Are Kelly and her husband back home?"

"Yes, she's been checking in on you, wanting to make sure everything's okay. She'll be back for the opening of Moonlight and hopes you can spend some time together. She really admires your work."

"I always knew she was a nice lady."

Jared laughs softly as he suddenly spins me around, catching me just in time to keep me from falling, and pulls me to him again.

I look up at him, and he maintains eye contact. I feel a connection as deep as when we made love. God, how I long for him to take control of my body again, but I don't want to spoil this moment. It's just me and him now, and as I hum the song, he watches me as if I'm going to give him the concert of his life.

"I'm really looking forward to when you sit down to play guitar and sing for me, but I don't want to rush you."

I lean my head on his chest, tuning into the rhythm of the music and the rapid beat of his heart.

"Your heart is beating so fast," I whisper.

"I know," he clears his throat, and I chuckle.

"Jared?"

"Yes?"

"Your voice is my favorite song."

Jared

The week is flying by, and I had to convince Cage to stick around for the festival next weekend. It was easy to convince him once he heard about the beer-drinking competition and Danny signing up.

I should be scared of the consequences, but who am I to lecture them? No way. I'd rather just laugh at their silly antics.

"Okay, thank you, Dr. Jacobson. No, I won't bother you anymore," I reply.

When I hang up, Hartley is watching me from the couch, scratching her head under the bandage.

"Don't hurt your ears, Poppy."

"I'm so itchy. I can't wait until Monday to take this off," she grumbles, and I pat her leg. Her toes are painted a pretty pink now, I could eat them up.

"Only two more days. I'm heading to Moonlight for a meeting, and then I'll be back, okay?. In the meantime, I recorded a few episodes of Hotel of Hearts for you to watch while I am gone."

"Oh, yeah! Sounds good."

"Did you look at Sawyer's plans?"

"He still hasn't shown them to me. Maybe he'll finally bring them over today. What did you talk to the doctor about anyway?"

"I asked him if we could have sex."

Hartley covers her mouth.

"You didn't!"

"Oh, but I did. And he said it was no problem. Of course, the rough stuff will have to wait, but the point is..." I walk over and lean down. "As soon as I get back, I'm going to spoil every inch of your body. Understand?" I seal the deal by lightly biting her lower lip, which tastes like cherries thanks to her lip balm.

I watch her eyes light up with excitement.

Damn, this is going to be a long morning.

"Hey, Jared?" she says, fidgeting with the remote. "Why are there three hockey games after three episodes of Hotel of Hearts?"

I may have downloaded some old games for her to watch. I want to get her more into hockey. For the first time in my life, I really want a woman to get excited about my game.

"Have fun, baby," shooting her a wink as I head for the door.

*

"We also need to stock up on strawberry wine because the girls loved it," I tell Jenna's father, who runs an excellent wine store.

"Okay, son. I've already arranged for the orchard to deliver fresh produce to the kitchen on specific days."

"It's great that we're doing so much with food and drink, but now we're way behind on the creative work," Boyle sighs. "With Hartley being out for a while, it seems to be holding the others back."

"Sawyer's doing his best."

"I wanted to talk about that. Couldn't you have a brother who wasn't such a jerk?"

"Are you afraid of a little competition?" my brother says from the corner, bouncing a rubber ball off the wall.

"Come on, please."

Their constant bickering during my video call with buyers makes the morning feel endless. Surprisingly, I'm finding it rather enjoyable. I've always liked working with architects, and now I get to let my bossy side out, which isn't half bad.

*

We meet up with Cage at Ryker's Cafe, where I'm relieved to be greeted warmly. It seems they've noticed how serious I am about Hartley.

"So you're asking me for sex advice," he leans back, pleased.

"No, I just wanted to let you know that I won't be available because I'm hopefully having a sex marathon with my girlfriend."

"You're a dirty dog, my friend."

"I wanted to meet you to ask if you'd like to watch the high school team with me before the festival. They're having some kind of celebration game, and the old coach wants me to see them."

"Sure, sure. I like the town, by the way. I've been able to check it out more since Jason and Marleen went home."

"Sorry, I haven't been around much to play tour guide."

"I'm not. I've finally had time to relax," he winks. "Listen, I have to go home tomorrow, but I'll be back for the festival, okay? I have some paperwork to take care of."

"Well, now you sound more excited. But, I won't get my hopes up."

"You're damn funny. Believe it or not, the Alaskan air was good for me, too. Even Jason's was too active... Man, the walls were thin in that cabin."

I laugh out loud.

"Okay, before you go, come over for poker tonight. I was thinking of inviting Hart's brother Danny and Eric."

"I'm in."

We talk for another hour, sipping our espresso coffees. When Cage says he needs to head to his cabin to finish packing up because he's leaving at dawn, I throw the money on the table. I wave to Ryker, who gives me a nod. I think he's starting to like me.

The sun's warmth kisses my skin, and I soak up the vitamin D.

"Well, if you'll excuse me, I've got a gorgeous woman waiting for me at home, so I'll see you at seven. Not a minute earlier, okay? Seven sharp."

"God forbid I spill my secrets to you."

Hartley

Jenna stopped by for a visit while Jared was at work. We watched three Gilmore Girl episodes and discussed Luke and Lorelai's relationship. We watched all the episodes Jared had recorded for me, and then we finally dove into watching Jared's games.

Since then, we've been glued to the screen, desperately searching the internet for the rules. Eventually, we gave up and simply watched these guys battle it out on the ice.

Jared plays an incredible game, but sometimes he gets so intense and angry that I can't help but wonder, is this really the guy I'm dating? Something must be wrong with me because when he gets into a scuffle over a rough hit and tosses his helmet aside, his damp hair falling into his face as he takes down his opponent like a Roman warrior, it...excites me. Jenna, too, seems equally mesmerized, fanning her flushed face after a while.

"How have we never watched NHL games together before?" she turns to me. "I mean, okay, they're hot, and those offensive plays, man! But it's a great sport. So thrilling! I wonder who'll win."

"Jenna, these are last year's games, you know that, right?"

"Shh, don't ruin the fun," she tosses a bag of popcorn into her mouth. "Cage isn't bad to watch play either."

"Well, well, well. I hear you've been avoiding him."

"I've never been into jocks, and he keeps eyeing me like he expects me to fall into his lap. Not a great first impression," she looks at me. "But he's cute," she grins.

"I heard he's leaving tomorrow but will be back for the festival. Jared wants to convince him to stay in Alaska."

"The only thing better than this is being a coach on the sidelines," she points to the screen.

After two games, I decide to call the clinic. I want to say thank you again and confirm my appointment time for Monday.

"I'll be right back."

I head to the kitchen, and when I finally get through to the nurse I've spoken with before, I relax.

"Miss Knight, everything okay?"

"Everything is perfect. I just wanted to express my gratitude for the opportunity, and I hope the rest of your surgeries went smoothly."

"Dr. Jacobson didn't have any other surgeries scheduled; you were his only patient. He flew out here just for you."

"What?"

"He was paid a significant sum for a special case that involved you. But I can't disclose who hired him, confidentiality agreement and all that."

"Oh, I... thank you. Okay, I understand. See you tomorrow then."

"See you at eight."

I return to the living room to see that Jenna is still focused on the game from her spot on the couch.

"Oh my God, did you see that puck twist? He really twisted it!" Then she turns to me, the smile fading from her face. "What's wrong?"

"Nothing... I spoke to the clinic, and they said Dr Jacobson had no other patients besides me. So why did the email say the doctor had a full list, and I was moved to the top?" Jenna looks at me suspiciously. "Do you know anything about this?"

"I'm not the one to tell you."

"Someone paid Jacobson a lot of money to come here just for me, and..." Then it all clicks in my head.

By the time Jared returns home, I'm not just excited about hockey; I've been reflecting on the summer's events so far and how we reached this point. I started tallying up when he started hiding things from me, and I realized it might have begun when we first got together. What does that mean?

"Hey, Poppy," he enters the living room, pleased to see one of his games on TV. "So you watched it. Awesome!"

"Jared."

"What?"

"I talked to the clinic."

Suddenly, he tenses. I wait for him to explain, but he stays silent. The silence speaks volumes.

"I learned some interesting information: There was no waiting list. Someone paid Jacobson a substantial sum to come to Alaska for my procedure," I sit up straight. You... it was you, wasn't it? You paid for my surgery." Tears gather in my eyes. "Why?" I ask softly.

Jared steps closer, bridging the gap between us as I hold my breath, waiting. He brushes my hair back, and his fingers find my racing pulse.

"You really don't know the answer?"

Without hesitation, I rise on my toes and kiss him fiercely as my fingers intertwine in his tousled hair.

I press against him, and he accepts everything I offer. His hands grip my hips, and as I reluctantly pull away, he looks at me with a hunger that ignites my desire.

I want him desperately, but I watch as he releases my hand and settles onto the couch. He gazes into my eyes, spreading his muscular thighs, silently inviting me. I step between his legs, hooking my fingers into his waistband and slowly sliding them off.

He watches me with dark eyes, exuding a mixture of coolness and heat. Jared is sex personified, and not just in this moment. He naturally emanates sensuality, and I find myself utterly captivated by him.

"Come here, Hartley," he murmurs in a husky voice. "You can do whatever you want to me."

Oh my God!

I feel the wetness between my thighs and the blush creeping up my neck, and I'm on the verge of collapsing. Thank God he's here, and I'm about to piece myself back together.

Jared

I don't remember ever wanting a woman as much as I do right now. Probably because this is the first time.

I watch as she slowly slides the cream-colored fabric down her silky, tanned thighs, her green eyes holding me in their gaze. Her breasts are visible through the thin white t-shirt, making my mouth water.

"Come closer" I lean back and watch her perfect figure. "You are so fucking sexy." Soft mounds, plunging nipples. Moisture glistening on her inner thigh. I want to fuck her... But for now, I'll control myself.

Okay, this is not going to work. I grab her thigh, pull her closer to me. I run my hand over her smooth skin, and when my fingers reach her wet pussy, I groan.

"Fuck, you're so wet... That's mine, isn't it? Every fucking inch of it is mine."

I circle her pussy, applying pressure to her most sensitive spot. Her face is flushed and her eyes are misty.

"Jared..."

"Ride me, Hartley! But first" I say. "Open your mouth!" She looks at me in surprise. "Hartley!" And she does.

I slide two fingers into her hot mouth. "See how fucking good your taste?" She moans in a strangled voice.

"Good girl!" And then it happens.

Hartley kneels down and watches me the whole time as she frees my cock from my pants. I watch her tensely and have to restrain myself from pulling her on top of me. Hart strokes my length and I close my eyes for a moment. But I have to see her! I want to see her take my cock in her mouth. She licks her tongue over me, then her perfect lips close around me. I grip her red hair tightly and dictate the rhythm. My hips rise. She slowly caresses me, but I dictate a faster pace. And when she looks at me with those big green eyes, I pull her away from me and pull her on top of me.

"I wanna fuck you, Hart! "

Hartley slowly kneels on either side of my hips and descends upon me. My jeans stretch painfully as her breasts rub against mine, and I can feel her nipples growing harder with each passing moment. Finally giving in to temptation, I slide my hand under the fabric and take her in my grip.

The moan I elicit from her reaches my groin. I lift my hips slightly to free myself from my jeans, and I may look a bit of a slob sitting there with my pants halfway down, but I don't care. Not when my fingers run along her thighs, and I feel the wetness beginning to pool between them. Her pussy rubs against me slowly and rhythmically. My cock is so hard I'm afraid I'm going to explode.

"God, that feels so good," I moan into her skin as I nibble along the curve of her neck, caressing the sensitive skin with slow kisses. "I want to be inside you!"

"I want you too," she sighs. "It's been too long."

At least I am not the only one who feels this way.

I stroke her wetness a few times, and I can tell she's ready for me. My pride swells knowing she is wet for me. I slide a finger in, then out, spreading her wetness, causing her to moan wantingly. Then I dip two fingers in slowly, urging her to move. Hart chases the relief slowly, then with increasingly impatient movements. "Come, Hartley, come on my fingers," I pant into her ear. "I want to feel your release grip me tightly." I curl my fingers to caress her g-spot, and she climaxes with shuddering breaths; I pull my hand away and kiss her.

I reach over to the dresser, pull open the drawer, and shake out a foil bag. Hartley takes it from me, ripping it open slowly to tease me before sliding it onto my aching erection. She climbs on top of me, placing a knee on both of my sides while she stares at me seductively. Lining her entrance with my cock, she slowly descends onto me, blowing my mind.

I slide into her hot, wet lips, grabbing her hips to control the rhythm so I can pleasure her from the best angle possible. I pull her to me and kiss her cherry-flavored lips. I soak in her essence and all she gives me. The sound of crackling skin fills the room, the scent of sex fills the air, and then, unable to contain myself any longer, I begin to rhythmically lift my hips to fill her even deeper. I want to feel everything and shatter her with pleasure just so I can put her back together again.

"I'm going to come," she screams softly between two lustful moans.

Our bodies cling together, I continue to suck and taste her lips, and then we slam into each other at a faster and faster pace. I pull her on top of me and take control, causing her to let out the sexiest moan, letting me know she is enjoying this new angle.

Heat rushes down my spine, and as she squeezes around my cock, I know she's about to keel over in euphoria. Her familiar panting and the trembling of her thighs make me explode, and I come with such intensity that I feel completely spent.

She leans against me, out of breath, and I hug her, gasping for air.

"Well then... we'll take a short break to eat and go for another round until the boys arrive," I say.

"You're impossible," she chuckles.

And who exactly turned my world upside down? I blame her.

Hartley

I have the sandwiches ready by the time the boys get here. I've already ducked into the room to work on my plans for The Moonlight because I don't want to disturb them, even though Jared asked me to be there. I think he's just using me to distract the boys to make it easier for him to win. He's a cheeky one.

I spread the last of my sandwich with avocado cream while hunched over my laptop. Jared's voice enters my head. "Poppy," I smile and continue singing quietly. "Poppy, hey! Poppy, poppy, poppy, poppy," he sings like a child. "Poppy, poppy, poppy!"

"What?" I turn suddenly to meet his worried gaze. He purses his lips and touches his hair thoughtfully.

"Jared, what is it?" I step up to him.

"I thought you couldn't hear me."

A weight of guilt hangs over me for a split second. "God, I'm sorry," I shake my head. "I just wanted to focus on my work, I'm sorry."

"No, no, I just need to get used to it," he sighs.

"Do you want to talk?"

"I..." he looks behind me. "Is it a tomato and avocado sandwich?"

"Yeah, but don't worry about it right now."

"That's my favorite," he snaps, his nostrils flaring with a sharp intake of breath.

This guy and his stomach...

"Jared, would you like a sandwich while we sit down and talk about why you're so freaked out?"

"If you insist," he smiles, and I roll my eyes and put two sandwiches on a smaller plate. I push them in front of him, and I reassure him about what he just said while he eats. He tells me how scared he is and that he needs time to adjust. I tell him that he is not alone and he tells me that my cooking definitely has a good effect on him. We manage to end the subject, and all is right with the world as the boys settle in.

"I really love your hair, Poppy," he slides his fingers gently through my hair.

"Really?"

"Yeah, this is so red now..."

"What?" I study my hair. "I am brunette. Maybe light chestnut... I think."

"No, your hair is a mix of colors. Honey, chocolate, and red. So much red under the light. And these freckles... You're a redhead, babe."

I think I'm getting to know my look and feel again through his compliments...

*

I wrap myself in a blanket and work on my designs while sinking into Jared's new mattress. It feels like I'm sitting on a cloud as it molds to my shape and embraces me like a luxurious hug. Lucretia licks herself next to me, sometimes adding a whine to my work as if to critique me.

The project has come a long way in the past week, and the decorators have already begun their work. There are still some finishing touches to be made, and I have to admit that Sawyer has done wonders with my design. He kept the Nordic style completely intact, adding bookshelves in the little nook in the corner and designer chairs in the other two corners. He drew on the Scandinavian feel. You'll find books on every theme, and the whole thing has a candlelit, relaxing corner vibe. It's a perfect match for the interactive snow wall, where tourists can view the Alaskan forest and mountain scenery through the windows, accompanied by a book and hot chocolate.

I'm working on the design when I notice that the house is quiet, with deep voices coming in from outside.

I can't believe Jared did this for me. He flew in the great doctor and literally gave me the sounds and the music back. My heart is pounding when I think about it again. I was so excited I didn't even notice the signs. How did I not figure it out sooner?

He asked me. He didn't say a word, but in every movement, in his voice, in his gaze, I could feel the same consuming desire and deep feeling that had been with me since he set foot in this room.

I hear a knock on the door and see Jared leaning against the doorframe, looking at me with a twinkle in his eye. "Hey, Poppy. Want to watch me beat the shit out of your brother? There's cocoa outside."

I'm curious to see how this plays out. "Hell yeah," I throw off my blanket and follow him down the hall.

"We moved the party to the backyard because Danny brought Cuban cigars."

"Great."

Before we step outside, Jared grabs my arm and pulls me toward him. His fingers gently brush the back of my head as he slowly kisses me. His touch is so soft that I pull away in a daze.

"What was that for?"

"Because I felt like it," he smiles, his eyes sliding down to my bare feet, or more specifically, my lacquered nails. "Cute."

I slip on my flip-flops and follow him into the courtyard, where the guys are playing cards at the cozy little wooden table. Cocoa is chomping away among the boys, and Sawyer is petting him like a puppy. I'm definitely going to have to talk to him about this. Most of the sandwiches I made, along with the IPA beer, have already been destroyed.

Jared opens a non-alcoholic beer for me and I grab it. The cold drink is refreshing on a warm night like this.

"Your brother told me he played baseball in high school."

"Oh, he was the best. He coaches the high school team. You'll see him around the school if all goes well."

"Things are going well because I'm staying," he looks at me seriously.

Wow, okay. Then it's really settled.

"Hey, Sawyer. You know what? I like your design plans," I wink at him. "I'm still working on it, but I think Boyle will like it, too."

"If I have my way, he'll like everything," he mutters.

"Sis, Mom, and Dad are really excited about the festival. I hope you know you have to help out. It wouldn't be fair for them to only me this year," he looks at me meaningfully. "Besides, they're always nagging me about how you're doing, like I've seen you a lot lately."

"Caleb, I always worked at Mom's cookie stand, if you don't remember. You were usually off with some girl or hiding in the maze with her, and you would always emerge in questionably disheveled attire after an hour or so," I reply.

"Okay, I'm just saying," he mutters. "And I haven't done anything like that since I was nineteen."

"You were with Janice Anderson three years ago, but that's unimportant."

"You were with Anderson," Danny looks at him in surprise. "Nice."

"Totally in love with her. He even cried when she left Alaska."

"I didn't cry. I told you my allergies were acting up."

Jared watches us, lost in thought. "So, big party this weekend, huh?"

"You have no idea," I say. "I'm sure Mom's got you on the list to work at the stand too."

"More hands on deck, more income," Caleb chimes in.

I glance around and spot Cage sipping a beer on the beach, enjoying the tranquility of nature. Leaving the guys behind, I head over to talk to him. Maybe I just want him to know I'm treating Jared right, especially after Meghan shattered so much trust.

I sit beside him, and he gives me a friendly smile.

"Thanks for letting us come over."

"This is Jared's house, but anytime."

"It's yours now, too. I hope you know that being here with him doesn't let you off the hook."

"I might not mind."

"It's a good thing you came out here because I actually wanted to talk to you," he says, turning to me. His blue eyes darken slightly, hinting at seriousness. I'm a little surprised, maybe a little scared, so I can't keep my mouth shut.

"Uh-oh, I hope you're not going to give me that line about not daring to hurt your friend, because I'm not," I explain. "He's so awesome, I couldn't ask for anything better, and I'm grateful for everything that makes me happy. Jared makes me happy."

Cage grins. "Two love-struck fools," he shakes his head. "But that's not what I wanted to talk to you about. It's more of a cautionary tale. I just want you to be careful."

"Of what?"

"The past," he frowns. "Jared thinks he's put the past behind him, but the media, if they get wind of what happened here, they can make a huge news story out of it. Besides, I know someone who would do anything to get him back in the spotlight."

"Who?"

"Meghan." My whole body tenses. I look back over my shoulder and see Jared playing poker with uninhibited laughter.

"Despite seeing how well Jared was doing without her, she never treated me well, even when she knew exactly how messed up she was. I don't know the exact details of what might have happened behind closed doors, and I don't want to pass judgment, but Meghan's actions can be purely selfish at times. So, I'm urging you to be cautious and watchful. You don't deserve the chaos that a media frenzy could bring."

Sometimes, I wonder what else I don't know about this woman, but I saw his pain when Jared talked about her and would never ask him directly. He had been hurt, lied to, and cheated on. A sense of dread washes over me, and I feel like this Meghan thing is far from over.

"I'll be careful, thank you."

"Don't sweat it. If anything goes down, you've got Jared in your corner. He'd take out any trouble before it even got close to you. He would have never done that for Meghan. Think about that," he winks and sips his beer.

I should be relieved since Cage just hinted that Jared's head over heels for me. But oddly enough, a weird tension knots up in my stomach, like a sense of trouble.

I can only hope that the shadows of the past in the form of Meghan don't interfere with our relationship.

Jared

I turned our post-boy's night cleanup into an impromptu date. Setting up a cozy picnic on the porch with sandwiches, drinks, and lavender candles, I wanted to create a romantic atmosphere. Hartley lay nestled between my legs as I gently caressed her neck, mindful of the bandage still covering it.

She snuggles up to me with a soft sigh, a satisfied smile on her face.

"It's so beautiful."

The water reflects the stars and the moonlight. The pines fade into the night, the mountains outlined behind them as if they'd been hand-painted.

"It's a sight worth seeing."

"I was talking about the guitar," she looks at me, and I notice the instrument propped up next to the chair.

"Well, since it's here, you might as well play it for me," I suggest, and she shoots me a nervous look.

"I don't know if I will be any good."

"I don't care. It's just us here."

"And Sawyer."

I look at the table where he's sprawled out. He is snoring loudly, but the blanket draped over him at least protects him from the cool evening breeze.

"What do you want to hear?"

She adjusts her position, cradles the guitar, and begins strumming. I request "Cannonball," the first song I heard her play. As the familiar melody filled the air, I couldn't help but be captivated by her presence and the raw emotion in her voice. Each note seemed to resonate with our surroundings, wrapping us in a cocoon of music.

"What?" she asked, catching me staring.

Without hesitation, I leaned in and kissed her passionately. "Could you be any more perfect?" I whispered, my heart overflowing with emotion.

Our moment was interrupted by my ringing phone, snapping us back to reality. With a sigh, I answered, greeted by the coach's voice on the other end.

As I wrapped up the call, Hartley looked at me with curiosity, and I reassured her confusion with a kiss.

"I have to go on a trip," I kiss her neck. A slight look of fear crosses her face. "Just for two days. I have to take care of something. A surprise."

"What kind of surprise?"

"For you," I suppress a smile. "A big one. I want you to be proud of me."

"I am proud of you, Jared."

"But this is different... I am going to do something good for a lot of people. And I want you to be really proud of me because I'm doing it all for you," I cup her face in my hands and kiss her softly.

I want to see her face as soon as I get back when I tell her the news. Then I'll ask her to move in with me for good because I don't want to let her go.

"Will you sleep with me at night now? Because I'm a little tired of you moving to the end of the bed to watch me."

I bite into her cheeky smile.

"I was just worried. But you don't have to ask twice."

*

The bandages came off on Monday, and yesterday, she went back to work at Moonlight. Everyone got her a cake to welcome her back, and she is in charge of picking the background music for work this week. I've never seen her so calm.

On Wednesday morning, as I left for my trip, leaving Hartley nestled in bed, I couldn't shake off a sense of anticipation mixed with nervousness.

I've already called an Uber so I can leave the Jeep here for Hart instead of having Danny bring it back from the airport.

I'll be in Montreal tonight with a connecting flight, and if all goes well, I'll be back tomorrow night.

When I'm ready, I go back to Hart's room, sit down at the end of the bed and lean in to kiss her. A little tired, she wakes up and wraps her arm around my neck.

"I have to go," I whisper. "I'll hurry back, okay?"

She nods with a smile as she stretches.

"Go back to sleep. Can I bring you back anything from Montreal?"

"Um... they have these yummy mint chocolate chip cookies at the airports. You could get me one of those," she says, opening one eye. I wrinkle my nose.

"Anything else?"

"Just yourself."

"Glad you got your priorities straight."

"Well, a mint chocolate chip cookie is a must."

"I get it." I kiss her again and want to go back to sleep, but I don't forget why I'm doing this. "I'm going now. Go back to sleep, Poppy."

Maybe I should be offended that she's asleep again the next minute like an exhausted little tiger with a soft snore coming from her lips.

*

In Montreal, everything happens so quickly. I have enough time to say a quick hello to my parents before I settle in at Grandma's for the night. I won't get to spend much time with Grandma either since I am only here for a quick trip.

Sawyer has already told everyone about Hartley. As soon as Hart is cleared to get on a plane, I'll bring her back and introduce her to my family.

I am meeting Coach and the head of the foundation at the Four Seasons restaurant and enter the lobby a little out of breath. I've had a strange chill since landing, so I take vitamins and aspirin to get me through dinner. I have no appetite, but I need to force something down my throat to keep my energy up. Coach Cole greets me with a big grin on his face.

"Good to see you, Zykov," he embraces me in his unique way.

"Thanks for the help, again."

"I should be thanking you for helping me. We've been considering starting a new foundation for a long time, and your idea is excellent. I've never thought of specifically assisting the hearing impaired.

"I have a muse, and I'm sure she will give me all the help I need to make this scholarship program perfect."

"Is everything okay with your girlfriend?"

"More than perfect. She's back at work this week."

"Good, very good. Come on," he taps me on the shoulder. "Let's go knock Ace Hamilton off his feet."

I get really excited as we walk into the restaurant. At our table sits a middle-aged man in a suit with graying hair, flanked by a young woman. Only this woman is all too familiar with her figure-hugging red dress and her upturned black curls. Familiar blue eyes find me, and I stop.

"I didn't know that she worked with him," the coach looks at me cautiously.

Yeah, me neither. Because then I wouldn't have come here to negotiate. Standing next to the future head of the foundation is my fucking ex.

*

"I must tell you, Jared, this foundation grant is fantastic. What inspired you?"

I push the salmon around my plate like it's the most disgusting meal. My stomach is churning, and I should be proud of myself for getting through dinner without looking at my bitchy ex. I have no idea what kind of game she's playing by showing up with Ace. I'm guessing the redneck hockey player she cheated on me with is long gone.

"I have a good influence in Alaska. I've met some great people there."

"When did you get such a big soul?" Meghan looks at me cheekily, and I just shake my head. The tension builds between us.

"I've always been generous with money, especially to those who don't deserve it," I say, and she suddenly tenses up and sinks back in her chair.

"Jared will be a part of our foundation from Alaska. He's spearheading significant projects out there." "He will also be coaching a high school team starting in September."

"I thought you were staying in the NHL," Meghan says, surprised, but I ignore her.

"I am surprised how long the waiting lists are for hearing-impaired people to receive services. I want to help as many people as possible get the right treatment. If this goes well, we could take the funding in other directions."

"That's great, Mr. Zykov. That sounds like an exciting project. My niece was born hearing impaired, but today's technology has greatly helped her".

"I also thought we could start sign language classes, like crash courses for family members."

Coach Cole looks at me with pride and nods at how well the conversation is going. Until Meghan pushes her chair out of the way and stands up.

"Excuse me, gentlemen, but since Jared is an old friend of mine, I'd like to borrow him for a few minutes. Would that be a problem?"

I watch her tensely, having no idea what she's up to.

"Please," she whispers.

Maybe I should speak up. I could unload all the chaos she's caused me, and then she can walk away with a patronizing "I'm sorry for everything." That sounds like a good option, so I clear my throat and stand up.

"Excuse me, we'll be right back."

I follow Meghan to the Four Seasons entrance, and as we step out into the cold evening, she suddenly turns to me.

"I want to talk to you, talk some sense into you."

"Excuse me?"

"You're denying yourself some really good opportunities, Jared."

"Because you're so interested, huh? I'm sorry, but you're not getting my money anymore," I said.

She looks at me like I hit her.

"I never cared what you did for a living. I cared about our relationship."

"No! Not that! Don't lie to me. I was the one trying to hold our already shaky relationship together while you ran off with my rival, Meghan!"

"I made a mistake, I know! But I'm not the only one who makes mistakes. Are you really staying in Alaska? Why? For a woman?"

I don't answer, and suddenly she laughs.

"You're not serious. You're really giving up the opportunity of a lifetime for a girl? You'll be coaching a kids' team, and who knows what else to fill your time? You could have a real career here after your sports career, Jared."

"But I'm happy, damn it!" I exclaim. "This is who I want to be. I'm not my money, I'm not my hockey career, and I'm not the Jared Zykov the media created."

"You can be who you want to be here, too," she chimes in quietly. "We were good. Everything was good before."

I can feel my head spinning, and I'm dizzy.

"Stop it! And besides, aren't you into 'old' money now?"

"You're an asshole," she looks at me incredulously. "Maybe I'm just ready for a mature relationship."

I snort.

"I'd believe you if I didn't know you're a sleazy snake. How many times did you try to get back at me after we broke up? You could have moved on but couldn't stand it when I was doing well without you."

"No... that's not true," she snaps.

"I'm done. I'm done. I'm done, and it's time for you to finally get it through your head. I'm not coming back," I declare.

"God damn it, stop it," she shouts at me, then suddenly presses herself against me and kisses me.

Well, almost. My whole body freezes, but just as our lips touch, I push away, maybe a little too forcefully, then lean against the wall of the Four Seasons and, in one well-aimed motion, throw up from the corner of the building.

"That's classy," she grumbles.

Someone helps me to my feet and I see the worried look on Coach's face.

"Are you okay?"

"Yeah, pretty shitty."

"I'll take you home. Meghan?"

"What?"

"Get out of here!"

Hartley

I cycle through the poppy field in the morning with a big grin on my face. The smell of the fresh air and flowers is incredible. The sound of birds chirping, cars in the distance, and flowing water brings out my inner Tina Turner. "The Best" plays softly from the basket speakers, making me feel like a rock goddess.

I sing along softly, swaying on my bike, which Jared just recently oiled. My bike can take it. Suddenly, I stop and hug the handlebars like they're my child.

"I missed your voice so much," I sigh into the basket speakers.

Turning sideways, I get lost in the sea of poppies and climb off the bike, dazed. I almost wade into the swirl of flowers, spinning wildly to the music. I lose my balance, causing me to fall into the field of poppies. Laughing out loud, I form a poppy angel and ignore the sound of a car until it stops on the dirt road. The door opens, and someone runs toward me. When I open my eyes, Sawyer is leaning over me, holding his phone to his ear.

"False alarm, she's still alive and looks fine."

"Who are you talking to?"

"No, I'm not calling an ambulance," he replies to whoever is on the other side of his call.

I suddenly sit up and watch in amazement as he hangs up the phone.

"Are you crazy? I was just lying in the flowers."

"Your bike fell over, and your legs were sticking out of the poppies. I was scared!"

I sit back and sigh.

"I just turned my brain off for a while. Today, I have to help my mom set up the booth before the festival."

Sawyer leans down beside me and exhales.

"Oh, yeah. The big festival. Jared and I have never been to one of those."

"No?"

He shakes his head.

"By the way, have you heard from him? He was supposed to fly back this morning, but no word."

"He texted me last night," I said, pulling my phone out of my jeans pocket. No, there hasn't been a message since. "Hey, can we put the bike on your flatbed, and can you give me a ride to the main square?"

"Sure."

On the way to the festival, I called Jared several times, but he didn't answer. I texted him in vain, but he didn't reply. He hasn't been reachable since last night. After Sawyer drops me off, I run through the booths being set up, oblivious to the voices around me. Jared gave me Cage's number, so I try reaching him. I find him at the carousel, sitting in front of the platform, absorbed in his phone.

As I approach from behind, I can see the photo he's staring at on his phone screen. A woman with dark hair kissing a man. Only she looks all too familiar. The man in the picture is my boyfriend, Jared!

As if sensing my presence, Cage suddenly turns and jumps to his feet.

"What was that?" I ask quietly.

"It's not what it looks like."

"So this picture isn't my boyfriend kissing another woman?"

"Yes, it is. I mean, no! Fuck," he rakes his hair. "One of my teammates sent it to me from the Four Seasons. He asked if Meghan and Jared were back together, which is a big no."

I step back, my legs shaking.

"I have yet to hear from Jared, but I know it's not what it looks like. Hartley, did you hear me? Meghan is a snake; she's obviously trying to start drama. Nate says Jared pushed her away immediately."

"Okay, well, that is slightly reassuring," I snort. "I haven't been able to reach him since last night."

Cage frowns.

"He would never do that. He would never do this to you. Please wait for him to explain before you jump to conclusions."

That would require actually getting him on the damn phone. But the worst is yet to come. I heard what people were saying in the town. It's not just a secret romance anymore; it's a full-blown love triangle.

'Is the dream couple back together?'

I can imagine Jared and Meghan are on the magazine cover.

'What about the girlfriend left behind in Alaska? Maybe Jared Zykov will never return to her.'

Jared

When I wake up for the third time, the sharp pain in my head has subsided, thanks to the herbal tea Grandma brewed in her apartment. With the help of Coach and Nate, my former teammate whose sudden appearance still puzzles me, I was practically carried to the couch in a haze. I must have taken something strong.

As I rub my face and groan, I reach for my phone and am greeted by a flood of messages and missed calls. Panic sets in.

"Don't fret, I've already informed everyone that you're under the weather," Grandma reassures me, appearing by the couch with her hands on her hips. Despite the sleepless night she spent tending to me, she looks remarkably composed in her worn-out jeans and Ramones band T-shirt.

"When was the last time you had a proper meal?" she asks, arching an eyebrow.

"I had a sandwich last night," I reply, my mind still foggy.

"When you met with Coach?" she prompts gently.

"No... wait, what day is it today?"

"It's Thursday, honey. Your flight was scheduled for this morning, but you were in no condition to travel. Thanks to my fantastic soup and charming personality, you're looking much better now," she quips, tilting her head to the side. "You can still catch the five o'clock flight. But eat something before you go."

"Good idea..." I murmur, my stomach protesting.

"I heard about the reconciliation with Meghan. I'm itching to hear all the juicy details," Grandma continues, unperturbed by my disheveled state.

"Don't hold your breath..." I mutter, mentally kicking myself.

"I can't believe you're starting a foundation. You truly are my grandson. Oh, and I had a chat with Hartley. I don't know what happened between you two, but she sounded rather tense. Did you have a falling out?" Grandma's question brings me back to reality.

"What? No!" I protest, feeling a surge of guilt.

I open Cage's texts, and my heart sinks as I realize the magnitude of the situation. Shit, shit, shit!

Throwing off the covers, I scramble to text Hartley, but there's no response.

Nothing happened, baby! I swear!

Okay, maybe not the best choice of words.

I'll explain everything once we're back home.

One more thing.

I'm getting you mint chocolate chip cookies.

Yeah, real smooth! Trying to explain away a misconstrued photo. I'm going to have to talk with Nate, although I know he meant no harm. I can only imagine how Hart must be feeling right now. I just hope she listens to my side of the story and doesn't break up with me.

"I knew it," Grandma says with a knowing smile. "I knew from the moment you two met that this was it."

"Am I becoming a hopeless fool?" I ask, feeling utterly defeated.

She shakes her head.

"A hopeless fool in love."

Hartley

In the dimly lit living room, still rocking my PJs, I tiptoe across the floor for a glass of water. But even after my chat with Candace, I'm nowhere near calm. I need to hear Jared's side of the story. But what really has me in a foul mood are those damn articles. That woman ensured everyone knew about Jared's 'good deeds' in Alaska, helping the poor hearing-impaired girl. Despite Cage giving me a heads-up, the media's twisted take makes me sick. I can't stand how they're painting me with pity, as if I'm just some stand-in for the former NHL star. It's just too much to stomach.

The door slams shut, and I freeze. Jared strides into the kitchen, breathless and coughing. His shoulders slump as soon as his eyes meet mine.

"Hi," he sighs.

"You cut your hair!" I blurt out in surprise.

His once unruly locks have been trimmed to just above his ears. I gaze down, spotting the bag of cookies in his hand. My traitorous heart quickens its pace.

"Yeah, Grandma insisted I get a trim at her friend's place before the trip," he nervously explains. "Hart, I..."

"I saw the picture."

"I know. It's not what it seems. I didn't kiss her!"

"So your ex spontaneously landed on your lips?"

"Yes! I mean, no! We were arguing, and out of nowhere, she kissed me. I pushed her away. Then... I puked all over the place."

I nearly chuckle at his boyish embarrassment, recognizing the sincerity in his eyes.

"There are witnesses if you doubt me..."

"I believe you."

"Really?" He appears taken aback.

"Your coach called me."

"Jesus."

"Is it true you're... starting a foundation? For me?"

"Yes. I wanted to surprise you."

"Oh, Jared. I'm speechless."

He steps closer, his icy hands enveloping mine.

"Don't say a word, please. This is for you, for us. Meghan is involved with the foundation's head. That's why she was there. I was furious, but I thought maybe I could finally find closure. Looks like that plan backfired," he scoffs. "My PR team is scrambling to appease the media before anyone creates chaos."

"It was terrifying," I confess. "The things they insinuated in this town... Do you know how agonizing it was? To have everyone think you were back together and I was just a stand-in?"

"But none of it's true! It was always you, Hartley. Always. My feelings for you haven't changed. Please tell me you still feel the same. If you have any doubts, tell me! I'll do whatever it takes to reassure you."

"I feared you might have a change of heart. That this mess might drive you away," I shake my head. "Did you know I dreamed about the accident after the surgery?" I swallow hard. "Where I was fleeing from Brody. Except, I wasn't running from him. I was chasing after you. But you turned your back on me, and I couldn't reach you..." I shake my head, the air in the room growing heavy, Jared's pained expression etched in my mind. "It's just a silly dream... Perhaps it merely reflected my insecurities."

"Poppy, I would never abandon you. And I'm about to prove it even more if you let me! You enchanted me from the moment I laid eyes on you. Giving you the gift of hearing was the greatest joy of my life, and now, I want to extend that to others. I've never felt more complete than I do here with you."

"You... you are so adept at apologizing. But I trust you."

"Good! I've been practicing," he grins. "Please forgive me for putting you in this position."

"I missed you," I sigh.

"I missed you too," he tilts his forehead against mine. "But... I should sleep on the couch tonight."

I tilt my head back in disbelief.

"What?"

"I don't want you catching whatever bug I have," he shakes his head.

"Oh, alright... well then," I step back.

"I'm going to take a quick shower."

I nod, watching him turn away. His movements seem strained, as if he's using every ounce of willpower to resist leaning against the counter. I won't deny I've been anticipating his return, even yearning for it. I've been craving sex, damn it.

Yet, I'm still... afraid. I'm afraid Meghan might discover where we live and who I am. I'm afraid I'll snap if the media uncovers my identity. I'm afraid it'll break me, and Jared will leave me out of fear. I know he's trying to protect me by keeping his distance. I just hope it doesn't come to that, but I can't shake the feeling that the photo and the articles are just the beginning.

Half an hour later, Jared is making his makeshift bed in the living room, and I lean against the wall, arms crossed.

"Are you really sleeping out here?"

"I don't want to risk getting you sick," he stands up straight. "Consider it my punishment."

"Punishment?"

"Yeah, I brought this storm upon us, so I'll weather it," he replies.

"Jared, it's not your fault," I sigh.

"My ex kissed me. For a split second, barely a peck, but she did. I pushed her away, of course, but that still didn't save us from a media frenzy," he reassures me.

As if seeking validation, he lingers.

"Okay," I shrug, heading to the bedroom, trying to banish the wretched image of them together from my mind. Today has been a whirlwind of emotions, to say the least.

I toss and turn in bed, leaving the door ajar in case one of us caves. I can hear the sofa creak with each movement. Just as I'm about to drift off, the wooden floor creaks, and the mattress dips under Jared's weight.

I feel the warmth of his chest against my back, and a sigh escapes me as his lips find the spot between my shoulder and neck.

"Hartley," he murmurs softly, and I reach back, running my fingers through his hair.

"Don't stop," I breathe. "Did I mention I like your new haircut?"

Jared chuckles softly, carefully turning me around to meet my eyes.

"I have two timelines. My old life, and you."

A poet, indeed.

"Jared..."

"I love you," he whispers, and I freeze.

"What?"

"I love you, Hartley Knight," he nudges my nose with his.

"Say it again," I plead.

"I love you," he kisses me but pulls back too soon.

"Once more," I whisper.

"I love you," he kisses my neck. "I fucking love you!"

With that, I roll onto my stomach, pulling him atop me, or at least trying to, but his muscles make it a challenge.

"Okay, this is new," he groans as he settles on top of me. "But I definitely like it."

"Gives us a way to have make-up sex, Mr. Zykov," I laugh softly.

I pull my shirt off, and he slowly pulls my shorts off. The touch of his fingers on my skin makes my skin burn.

I watch him over my shoulder, and when he sits over me again and spreads my legs with his knees, I gasp.

"Jared?"

"Yes?"

A slow smile spreads over my face.

"I love you too!"

The way his face lights up makes all the hard work worthwhile. His actions have already proven his love, but now that I have his words after all these years of silence, it surpasses everything.

He pulls open the drawer and takes out a foil packet. He slides the condom on and leans back on top of me before sliding his length inside me teasingly slowly.

He pins me to the bed with deep, long strokes.

"Damn, baby, you feel so good," he says, whispering in my ear. "Tell me what you want, baby."

I grip his hair harder and harder, and my lustful moans give him all the answers he needs.

He rests his arm beside my head while his free hand grips my hip tightly, pushing himself deeper into my center.

I can sense he's nearing his climax, and I'm on the brink of mine as well. He weaves his fingers with mine, eagerly seeking the sensation of fulfillment.

"Yes, yes, yes..." I gasp, throwing my head back, pressing my hips against him, taking it all in as I surrender completely.

Jared follows me through my orgasm with a loud grunt. We collapse together like a pair of exhausted marathon runners crossing the finish line.

"I'm not saying I want your ex to kiss you all the time, but I definitely don't mind the fights," I say breathlessly. Jared kisses my shoulder. I feel his chest tremble against my back as he laughs softly.

Jared

"Wow, well..." says Cage next to me. "These kids really need help."

That is not what I was hoping to hear.

Saturday is the festival's opening day, and East Morgan High is playing a "friendly" game against a team from another town. Clearly, "friendly" isn't in the other team's vocabulary because they're wiping the floor with us.

Both offenses had a fight so intense they could barely get off the ice. Our goalie let in three goals made by his teammates, and our defense was a complete mess. They were bumping into each other like they forgot they were on the same team.

Come September, I'll have a lot more work to do than just building this team from the ground up.

"Well, you could still stay and help me teach these kids how to play," I tapped him on the shoulder.

"Yeah, right!" he snorts.

"I'm serious. You are a licensed teacher, remember."

"I'm still thinking about it," he mumbles.

"And I suppose a certain fire-breathing Italian chick is an added bonus."

He tilts his head at me.

"Are you talking about Jenna?"

"I'm not talking about anyone; I'm just saying. There are a lot of Italian girls around here," I shrug.

"Yeah, I doubt she'd go for me, and frankly, I'm not crazy about her either," he says gruffly. I know he's lying. I know him like I know my own brother.

"I can convince you to move here."

"Good luck," he grins. I turn to see Jenna staring at us. She's looking at Cage's ass. She catches his eye when she sees she's been caught, but I stare back: I saw it!

And she raises her middle finger elegantly.

"Is Hartley okay?" Cage asks, and I turn back to the track.

"Everything's fine. The PR team is already at work. They're doing everything they can to keep her identity under wraps. It's not that we're keeping it a secret. We just don't want the media here right now."

"Makes sense. I'm sorry I let her see the pictures, brother. Can you forgive me?" his eyes flash at me.

"Yes."

"How many times?" He raises an eyebrow at me.

"A gentleman never talks about that." He smirks at me.

 "Three times," I grin.

"Oh, that's my buddy! You're one lucky guy," he laughs.

"Laugh all you want, but when it happens to you, I'll be the first to laugh."

"Dream on..."

*

I catch Hartley from behind at the cookie stand as she squeals. Her mother watches our stunt with amusement.

"Hi, Poppy," I kiss her cheek.

"Is the game over? How was it?"

"Terrible." Cage says bluntly.

"Not that bad," I say simultaneously.

"It took half an hour to get the guys to stop sliding around the ice like crazy ducks."

"But in the movies, the underdogs always win," she says with a wink. That's why I love her… She's always so optimistic.

"Jared," Hande says, hugging me. Before letting go, she whispers in my ear, "Thank you. I'll never be able to repay you." Seeing the tears in her eyes hits me hard.

"I'd do anything for your daughter, I promise," I reply sincerely. "Hey, babe," I say, grabbing Hart's hand, "let's head down to the apple orchard. We can get a basket and pick some apples."

Her eyes light up.

"Okay, okay, I'm about to take a break," she points at the delicious cookies, but her mom pushes her away.

"You go ahead. I'll hold down the fort."

Hart starts to walk away, but I grab her hand and pull her toward the Jeep.

"We're going here first. I brought someone with me." I catch a glimpse of a baby goat through the car window.

"Cocoa!" exclaims Hart. "You brought him?"

I open the door and pick the little guy up.

"I read about animal therapy. I thought it might help him be less antisocial."

"Goat therapy?" she asks, looking puzzled, then breaking into a slow, embarrassed grin. "You're unbelievable."

Even though she's teasing me, I can tell I've made her happy.

We place Cocoa with the other goats, and while he's initially scared, he doesn't have a panic attack. Soon enough, he befriends a spotted goat and, like a toddler, eagerly waits for us to leave so he can start getting into mischief.

I lead Hartley down the path to the apple orchard, where they're hosting apple picking as part of the festival. It's a great idea, especially seeing how happy it makes her.

"Hello, Matteo," Hartley waves to a middle-aged Italian man.

"Hey honey, are you picking apples too?" He hands me a white basket.

"Yeah, it was Jared's idea."

I shake Matteo's hand. "Nice to meet you, Matteo."

"My daughter told me about you."

"You must mean Jenna. She's a big fan," I reply.

Matteo laughs hoarsely. "Don't take her snarky attitude personally; she's just protective of her best friend."

"I get it," Hartley says with a wink. "I'd be cautious with any guy before trusting him with someone I care about."

"Should I be jealous? What exactly would you be looking for?" I ask, curious.

"Oh, you know, just testing them out to make sure they're good enough," Hartley teases.

I laugh as Matteo joins in. "Jesus, I'm just kidding. But I would definitely give you a thorough vetting."

"Like what?" I ask.

"Just basic stuff. Like what kind of toilet paper you use."

"What?"

"You can tell a lot about a person by the quality of the paper they choose."

I don't even want to know. We walk hand in hand through the trees, and when we find the perfect apple tree, I crouch down and lift Hartley onto my shoulders. Her hands tremble as she laughs and clings to my shoulder as I stand up.

"You better pick lots of apples, woman! I want a taste of your apple pie."

"You're welcome to my pie anytime, pretty boy," she responds with a chuckle, and I let out a soft groan. I certainly don't want to attract any unwanted attention while she's wrapped around me like this.

Hartley

As Jared heads off to grab a drink, I sit on one of the benches. My gaze wanders to the towering Ferris wheel, contemplating conquering my fear of heights. Maybe I could convince Jared to join me, although I know he's just as wary of heights as I am. I remember one morning when he looked like he might faint on a ladder. I was so worried that I even dragged out an old mattress in case he decided to bail.

Scanning the area, I notice an expensive-looking car pull up. A woman with black hair emerges, adjusting her dark glasses. Instantly, I recognize her.

Slowly rising to my feet, I observe as she approaches someone. Suddenly, the person gestures towards me. Like an approaching storm, she strides over, leaving me unsure what to do. Before I can consider my options, she's standing right in front of me. Towering over me by half a head, she regards me with a disdainful look that makes me regret my choice of attire—a simple white skirt paired with brown cowboy boots—compared to her regal blue dress. Meghan's taste in clothing is impeccable, after all.

"Hartley Knight?" she inquires.

"Meghan?" I reply, crossing my arms.

"Great, so you've heard of me. I hope only good things," she quips, the corners of her mouth twitching.

Damn, she thinks she is so funny.

"What are you doing here?" I demand.

"I want to talk to Jared, and I'm asking for your permission. I don't want another misunderstanding," she explains.

"Another misunderstanding? You mean like when you kissed my boyfriend?" I retort.

"I just wanted him to listen to me because he's being stubborn. I was foolish, and I apologize. But I need to talk to him," she insists. "He's being unreasonable."

"And why is that?" I challenge.

"Because he's passing up a golden opportunity," she replies.

"Jared can make his own decisions. It would be best if you accepted that," I assert.

"Then let's have a woman-to-woman conversation," she steps closer. "Do you want to be the one holding him back in his career? Because I've been in that position, and it's not pleasant."

"I'm nothing like you!"

"Sweet of you to think so. Maybe you are, maybe you aren't. But I'm certain Jared won't stay here for long. He's always been a wanderer. He falls in love with a place, a woman, and believes he owns it forever. But eventually, he grows tired of it all, because that's who he is," she explains.

I feel a knot form in my stomach, her words hitting me like a blow.

"If you're doing this because you want him back, it won't work. Even if I wasn't in the picture, it wouldn't change that," I counter.

"I don't want Jared back, but he was my friend, one of my best, and I care about him. Consider this my way of making up for the mistakes I've made. If not me, then at least he should find happiness," she says.

"Jared is happy, Meghan," I state firmly.

"He was happy on the ice," she retorts sharply. "Look, I just want a chance to talk to him and convince him. If he truly doesn't belong here, he'd better leave soon, don't you think?"

"What the hell are you doing here?" an angry voice interrupts from behind me.

Turning around, I see Jared's face twisted with rage, a sight I've never witnessed before.

"I'm just introducing myself to your girlfriend," Meghan replies coolly. "I need to talk to you."

"The hell you do! Get out of here, Meghan, or I'll consider it harassment," Jared snaps.

"Jared," I interject, touching his arm. "Maybe you should talk to her. Let's calm down."

"What?"

"Let's end this, Jared. It's not healthy for you," I urge.

"She's got a point," Meghan chimes in, earning a sharp glare from me.

Turning to Jared, I stand on my tiptoes and press a kiss to his lips, my hand brushing against his stubbled cheek.

As he finally begins to relax, returning my kiss.

"I'll be waiting right here, okay? Just talk to her and then tell her to get back on her broomstick and fly far away from here," I say.

The look on Meghan's face after our kiss is priceless. A heavy feeling settles in my chest as I walk away despite the satisfaction of leaving her behind.

Jared

"No!"

"Jared," Meghan moans. "Just consider it for a moment."

"I'm not going back, Meghan. You don't know me. You never really did. I've been here all summer, and I've never been more certain about anything. You have to understand I don't want to watch NHL games from the sidelines anymore. I'd rather start over because that's what I truly want!"

Finally, as if a realization dawns on her, she runs her fingers through her hair with a resigned sigh.

"Do you know how hard it was for me? You were never home, and I was always afraid you'd cheat on me because, let's face it, it's not uncommon during away games. It drove me crazy."

"And instead of talking to me, you cheated!"

"Because I thought you already had, and I wanted to hurt you before you hurt me," she sobs, quickly composing herself. I've never seen her so vulnerable. It's like she's shedding that icy exterior for a moment.

"Meghan..."

"I'm sorry! I'm sorry I hurt you! I just want to make it right by knocking some sense into you."

"But sometimes, the right way isn't the same as how others make it right for us," I say softly. "I want you to find happiness and be true to yourself. Don't let fame and money change you. Remember the girl you used to be. I know I made mistakes, too, but wasn't the money good for college? It made me smarter. What about you?" Meghan listens in silence. "Your happiness means everything to me. Why can't you do the same for me?"

She lets out a shaky sigh.

"Yes..." she tucks her hair behind her ears. "I... I issued a statement about the picture. I admitted it was a mistake and my fault. You pushed me away. It was just a moment of weakness. I hope that helps make things right."

"Thank you."

"That woman..." she starts a little judgmentally, but I cut her off.

"That woman is going to be my wife one day."

Meghan gives me a startled look, and even I'm surprised by what I just said. What the hell?

"Then I hope she's smarter than me," she smiles sadly, but before she walks away, she delivers one final blow. "She's going to ruin it, Jared. If you're not careful, she won't be able to handle what comes with being with you."

Well, thanks.

As I watch my ex walk away, I try to convince myself that Meghan is just trying to offer some advice, but it's hard. Is there truth to her words? Am I doing Hartley a disservice? How long before the hockey world finds out about us? If we don't keep it a secret, what then? Or have I truly moved on, and there's always another player the public will be more interested in?

I replay the summer events in my head, including the moments with Hartley and the conversations with Meghan.

Feeling anxious and uneasy, I head to Hart's father to have a talk. Maybe he'll think I'm crazy, or maybe he'll never forgive me, or maybe I simply don't care. After a brief conversation, he lets me go. I quickly hop into my car, leaving the festival behind without a second glance.

Hartley... she'll understand.

She has to understand why I left.

Hartley

Jenna and I watch in amazement as Danny and Cage battle it out in the beer-drinking tournament. Despite their evident struggle, they soldier on, determined to outlast each other. Maggie joins us, resigned to the inevitable consequences of Danny's drinking antics.

"If he thinks I'm staying up all night with him like last time, he's sorely mistaken," Maggie remarks with a hint of sarcasm.

As I finish my meal, I glance over to see Meghan hastily driving away. A sense of relief washes over me, hoping it signals the end of their stormy past. But my relief is short-lived as I spot Jared sprinting after her car. When he hops in, seemingly to follow Meghan, my heart sinks.

"Where's your friend off to?" Jenna inquires, noticing my concerned expression.

"That's Jared's ex," I reply with a heavy sigh. "I left them alone to talk."

"Are you serious?" Jenna's disbelief is obvious.

"They needed privacy," I explain with a shrug. "Guess they're hashing things out."

"What if he's chasing after her?" Jenna suggests.

"He's not going back to her," I assure her. "He must have some good reason for leaving."

"I'm not worried about him chasing Meghan," I admit. "I'm worried he might leave altogether. Is it selfish of me to want him to stay here instead of going back to the NHL?"

Maggie interjects, her tone firm yet understanding. "Jared never wanted to go back. He talked about settling here last year. You're not selfish for wanting him to be happy."

"Maggie's got a point," Jenna agrees.

"I'll step away for a bit so you two can talk. I don't want to watch Danny overindulge again." With that, Maggie walks away, giving us the space we need to have a conversation.

"Hartley," Jenna takes my hand. "You know I have a hard time letting people in, but I've taken a liking to Jared. He doesn't know it, and I'd like to keep it that way, but I like him because he's a good person. I want you to think about this rationally. The guy paid a fancy doctor to get your hearing back, and he's setting up a whole foundation just for you. A man who doesn't have a long-term view of his future with a woman and isn't idiotically in love doesn't do that."

"You're right," I smile, then hug her tightly.

I am a bit calmer now, but as the hours pass, my head is filled with worse and worse fears, I'm on the verge of a breakdown. I reach the final point around eight o'clock at night when Jared has been gone for four hours. No phone calls, no messages, nothing.

I'm standing in front of the Ferris wheel with Jenna, but no matter how much I try to convince her, she won't get on. She's been glaring at her phone for hours as if it personally offended her.

"It's eight o'clock," she grumbles again.

"I know, but since Jared's nowhere to be found, I'll do it alone," I nod firmly because I'm a brave girl or something.

"All by yourself?" the ticket guy asks when it's my turn.

"Yes," I say, getting into the open cabin. He buckles me in thoroughly. I have no idea how stable this ride is, but I hope my story doesn't end here.

"Let's go," he calls, but someone suddenly slams into the seat next to me before we start the ride.

"I'm going too," Jared says, out of breath. His face is flushed, and his hair is disheveled as if he had just run a marathon. The guy buckles him in, and when we start, I'm still watching him with my mouth open.

"What the hell, Jared? You're afraid of heights!"

"Sorry for keeping you waiting," he looks at me with a misty look. "And for throwing up on you because I'm scared shitless."

"What are you doing here? I thought you were gone. I saw you drive away and..."

"You didn't think I wasn't coming back, did you?" he asks quietly as we climb higher into the sky. "Please tell me you didn't think I was going with her."

"I wasn't afraid you'd go with her, but I was afraid you'd leave. I'm being selfish, aren't I?" I admit.

"Am I selfish for wanting you and not wanting to go anywhere without you? Or am I being selfish by leaving the NHL?"

"I'm sorry, it's just... Meghan made me insecure."

"Believe me, she's good. She didn't just do it to you. I really wondered if I was good enough for you." Before I can say anything, he interrupts with urgency. He clasps my hand tightly, his grip almost crushing mine. "And I've decided that I want to be the best for you. I've been thinking about this whole summer and the progress you've made for me. I finally understand what it means to be charitable." I answer with a piercing look. "Okay, that's the wrong way to put it. I mean what it feels like to help others. What it feels like to love new friends. What it feels like to be with the most perfect woman you could ever dream of."

"You're perfect for me, Jared Zykov."

He loosens his grip and looks at me like I'm the greatest gift in the world.

"I love you, Hartley. More than words can say. You're like air to me; I can't imagine life without you. You're everything I've ever wanted and more. When I saw this ring, I knew it had to be yours. It's a promise, a symbol of our love. If you want it to be just a gift, that's okay. But if you want it to mean everything, then let it be a promise of forever. Will you marry me?"

"I... I..."

"I don't expect an answer right away. Hart... I think, you are my soulmate, who I fell in love with too quickly, and it was scary. You can wear the ring for as long as you want. But I needed to take this step towards you. I love you more than anything. I want you with every fiber of my being. I want a future with you—Lucretia, Cocoa, and maybe even a little goat friend for him. I want children, our children. A family, a treehouse, maybe a small farm for the goats. I don't know all the details yet, but I know I want it with you. So, Hart, what do you say? Do you want this? Do you want me?"

Was there ever any doubt that Jared Zykov was the perfect match for me? No one else could compare, considering all he's done for me in just a few months, things others haven't managed in years. As his hopeful green eyes meet mine, the answer is crystal clear.

"I want it all!"

"Hell, yes," he leans into me and kisses me with a passion that I fear the teenagers below us are filming.

Someone whistles, and I look down to see a seventeen to eighteen-year-old boy and his girlfriend grinning up at us. It's only now that I realize we're at the top of the Ferris wheel.

"That's Coach Zykov!"

"Shut up!" he shouts back. "I have no idea who that is, but I think he's one of the team players," he mumbles. "Why are we stopping?" he gasps.

I turn his face back and kiss him deeply. I run my tongue along his lips, deepening the kiss as he lets me in.

I run my hand over his chest, but Jared takes mine and leads it to his nether regions.

"I have an idea how you can make me forget how high we are," he winks as he places my hand on his groin.

I catch my hand and slap his stomach as he moans in feigned pain.

"There are minors underneath us," I hiss, unable to wipe the embarrassed grin off my face.

"If you don't think they've ever done anything like this, I'd rather not tell you what it was like to be a high school hockey player on the East Coast."

Laughing, I lean into his lap, and he puts his arm around me. The view of the city and the forest is amazing.

"This dress looks fantastic with those cowboy boots, honey. I could easily reach under it if I wanted to," he raises an eyebrow. "No one will see."

I shake my head and sigh, but then I take his hand and place it on my thigh as I slowly spread my legs.

"Damn, you're killing me!"

Jared kisses the back of my neck as his hand slides along the inside of my thigh, and when his fingers find my white lace bottom, I bite into my lip, stifling a scream that wants to break out.

My fingers get lost in his dark waves as he caresses my sensitive skin. His fingers, unlike mine, are in a more intimate place. He traces slow, deep circles down my midsection through my bottom, and as he keeps pressing that sensitive spot, I gasp for breath.

"You're bad girl, Hartley," he brushes his lips across my ear. His raspy, deep voice has an effect on the area between my legs. "There are minors underneath us."

"God, stop it," I say heavily.

"Stop it?"

He pulls his hand away, but I jerk it back.

"Don't stop," I laugh.

He looks at me, his eyes dark and deep.

"I'll never stop, Poppy!" He presses a kiss to the scar behind my ear. "You're a real tiger, my love, and these are your tiger stripes. I don't know a stronger woman than you. So no, I'll never stop."

And he doesn't, as I melt into a sweet warmth, my heart racing. He takes me all the way to the top, my thighs trembling, and when the Ferris wheel finally resumes its ascent, Jared has shed his fear of heights and is instead beaming with satisfaction.

But I wouldn't have it any other way, I think to myself as I bask in the moment.

Epilogue

Hartley

One year later

I sink into the plush new sofa we bought two weeks ago, feeling like I'm in heaven. Jared's parents, Candace and Brianna, came for a visit because I wanted to share some big news. Well, that's not entirely true. I was actually seeking advice from his mom. Still, Brianna overheard, and within five minutes, Jared's dad was hugging me so tightly I feared he might crush my bones.

Brianna settles down beside me, flashing a grin and proudly displaying the jersey she hastily made for me earlier that day.

"Jared's going to be floored!" she exclaims.

The thought sends a shiver down my spine. But my heart races as I glance at the jersey and the writing on the back. I'm practically bursting with excitement, but I also feel a bit queasy; the nerves are kicking in. However, I definitely don't want to ruin Brianna's creation with an unexpected upheaval.

Since we met, Brianna and I have been fast friends, much to Jared's dismay. I'm forever grateful for those childhood photos of Jared.

Now, we're gathering before the big game. Jared spent six months coaching the local hockey team, and it was nothing short of miraculous when the boys clinched the championship. He then passed the torch to Cage and moved on to coach the college team, where he's been making quite a name for himself. Today, we're gearing up for an exhibition game featuring amateur and professional players, all to raise funds for the foundation Jared established last year. I've never been prouder of this man.

After Candace returned to Alaska, we relocated across the lake from Cage. We set up a small farm for Cocoa, who found a companion in Pooh last year. They practically grew up together, and it came as no surprise when they blessed our little family with some baby goats. Well, maybe it was a bit of a surprise, but it's clear they were smitten with each other from the start. I still recall the day we moved in and meticulously cleaned Grandma Candace's house, only to be scolded as soon as she walked through the door. "You think I don't know what you two have been up to here the past few months?" It was an awkward situation, though Jared quite enjoyed picking his grandmother's brain.

Jared's mother enters the living room.

"I adore this house," she sighs, then gives me a gentle pat on the cheek. "You've got a lovely blush, dear…"

"Please, Sylvia, spare the girl further embarrassment," Jared's dad chimes in, though not before Sylvia leans in to plant a few cheeky smacks on my face. It's like being a child again. All that's missing is having my face wiped clean with a licked finger. I almost expect it, given the way Sylvia scrutinizes my mascara with furrowed brows, but thankfully, her finger doesn't make it to her lips before I intervene.

"Ew, Mom, please behave," Brianna groans. "Dad, let's go! We're running late!"

Ivan dashes out from the dining room, decked out in Jared's old jersey and a Wild Wolves baseball cap.

"You do realize your son isn't on the WW team anymore, right?" Sylvia points out. "But it doesn't matter. What matters is showing support."

And she's right. So we finally hit the road, eager to avoid the rush of fans in town for the weekend. Unfortunately for McRoyal, there's a sizable crowd, and I'd rather not contend with zealous hockey enthusiasts.

*

Inside the rink, I sit beside Jenna, who's practically bouncing in her seat with excitement. I'm feeling a bit queasy from the early start—I may have inadvertently crushed a woman while vying for the last of the cheese nachos. Lately, I seem to find myself in too many food-related skirmishes.

We managed to snag a booth amidst the bustling crowd. However, I can already feel regret settling in after indulging in chocolate, nachos, and Coke. The nausea hits me once again, and I struggle to keep it at bay.

Danny and Maggie sit in front of us, casting knowing glances my way. It's as if they can read my mind.

"Here come the hotshots!" Jenna exclaims as the halftime show kicks off.

As the game resumes, Jared's team storms the ice. If I thought watching game footage was thrilling, seeing him play live is nothing short of awe-inspiring. He's cautious with his knees but plays with incredible skill.

"Number thirteen is really something," Jenna remarks. "Absolutely drool-worthy. Eric's going to be thrilled."

"Eric's married," I remind her.

"Please. Freddie had a wife and still went out with that waiter."

No argument there.

The game continues, and Jared maneuvers with finesse. He passes the puck to Cage, and I finally get to witness their teamwork firsthand.

Cage skillfully maneuvers the puck between his opponent's legs before passing it back to Jared. I hold my breath, fearing it might be a botched pass, but Jared strikes the puck with such force that it flies past the goalie and into the net.

He throws his hands up in triumph and the horn blares. Jared immediately locks eyes with me, pointing in my direction as a reminder of his promise to score three goals. Just one more to go.

As the game draws closer to the end, I feel the nerves creeping in, recalling Brianna's words. Her husband had stumbled in just minutes before kickoff, wheezing and breathless. That was enough to prompt Bri to regale me with all sorts of stories.

"I told him the big news, and he passed out. Thought he was dreaming. Then I told him again, and he passed out again."

Please, don't let me end up in the emergency room. I'll never live it down.

The rest of the hockey game is a whirlwind of excitement. I can barely remain seated as Jared charges toward the goal once more. Two opponents try to take him down, but he manages to pass the puck to Cage, who scores from an impossibly tight angle.

Jenna screams beside me.

Three goals down, but there could be more.

As the final buzzer sounds, all the wives and family members flood onto the ice, myself included. Jared makes his way over to me, taking my hand as he greets me with a kiss.

"Hi, Poppy," he says. "Did you enjoy the game?"

"You were incredible," I reply.

He chuckles before pulling me close. I hesitate to step onto the ice, fearing I might slip and fall, triggering a bout of nausea.

"Is that my jersey?" he asks, eyes widening with excitement as he takes in the sight.

"Not technically. I had it custom-made," I confess.

Emblazoned with the name of his middle school team and his number 27, the jersey fits me like a glove. I spin around, but my sudden movement nearly causes me to lose my footing. Jared steadies me, wrapping his arms around my waist.

"You're going to hurt yourself, sweetheart," he scolds gently, turning me around.

"What's this? Zykov? Daddy?"

When I turn back, I see a confused look on his face, followed by a sudden realization. His expression lights up with wonder as he shakes his head.

"Are you pregnant?" he leans in close.

"Good game, Daddy!"

Jared pulls me to him, then suddenly lifts me into the air and kisses me all over my face. When I look into his eyes, I see tears.

"No kidding? Seriously?"

"Seriously, seriously. It wasn't enough for you to get a prenup. You had to get me pregnant. Congratulations, your guys are atomic even with the condom."

Jared is grinning like he won the lottery, and so am I because, damn it, I'm happy to have the fruit of our union growing inside me.

I see Jenna coming toward us with Cage behind her. She's sobbing as she stomps towards me, a little unsteady as she holds the letter I left on her doorstep today. I told her to wait to open it until the end.

"Oh my God," she cries and hugs me. Her eyes are puffy, her nose is wet, and her face is so red that I'm afraid she's going to suffocate. "I'm going to be an aunt."

"I wrote her a letter from the baby."

"She got a letter?" Jared looks at me, stunned.

"I'm her best friend," Jenna sobs.

"God, Jenna, get a hold of yourself; if the baby sees you like this, he's going to be scared of you," Jared snaps back as he wraps his arms around me from behind, but the smile is still on his face.

"You're beautiful, honey," Cage kisses her cheek. They both teach at the local high school and last fall, they began a battle that turned into love. But that's another story. "Tell her she looks nice," Cage looks at us nervously, maybe a little worried.

I grin, lean my head against Jared's chest, and look up at him.

"I sure as hell hope you have a daughter, Jared Zykov," Jenna wipes her eyes.

The blood drains from my husband's face, and then he looks over at me as if he's weighing the odds.

"No way, I can't have a daughter!"

Jared

18 months later

Gliding to the edge of the rink, I find my beloved wife standing there, with our adorable, occasionally smelly, little one by her side. Despite the diaper changes, I wouldn't trade this for the world. As a dad, I feel incredibly fortunate. Today, we've arranged a family outing to the skating rink, and it's my turn to introduce our daughter to the joys of ice. Hartley's cheeks are rosy, her curls as enchanting as ever. Her mischievous green eyes meet mine as I approach.

Pausing in front of them, I scoop up our little bundle of joy. "Well, hello there," I playfully nudge her nose, eliciting a crinkle. "Titty," she grins her first word, a testament to her daddy's girl status.

"I'll take her for a spin," I tell Hart before whisking away with our precious princess. Despite occasional mix-ups in our routines, I cherish these moments. "You're quite the charmer, aren't you?" I muse as we skate. "You're already better at undressing Mommy than I am."

Cage joins us, lifting his son with a familiar expression. "You might want to have a word with your son. Savannah isn't allowed to date until she's thirty," I tease him.

"We'll cross that bridge when we're on vacation together, and they're sneaking into each other's rooms at seventeen," he quips before we skate off. I watch him, momentarily horrified by the thought. Surely that won't happen.

As Cage takes over with Savannah, I return to Hart, stealing a kiss before passing our daughter to her uncle. "Hello, beautiful," he greets her warmly.

My brother has flourished, thanks in part to the woman who captured his heart. Ever since Saw has been much more agreeable.

238

"Take good care of her. I'll take Hart for a skate," I tell Cage before winking at my wife, who steps onto the ice with a hint of shyness, but I'm here to hold her steady.

Skating backward, I pull her close, surprising her with a kiss. "Did you ever imagine it would be like this?" I ask.

"Marrying an ex-NHL player who claims the rubber broke because his guys are too strong? No, that wasn't in my dreams," she quips.

"Smartass," I playfully tap her nose. "And you? What about Alaska?"

"Never thought I'd fall for a guy who mistook me for a stalker and stripped half-naked in front of me the first time we met," she chuckles, her dimples reminding me of our daughter.

"I never thought you were a stalker!" I protest, earning a skeptical look from Hartley. "Okay, maybe I did. But I'm glad I did," I add, tilting my head toward her.

"What?" she asks, puzzled.

I kiss her again, then rest our noses together.

"Pretty perfect, isn't it? This *Chalet Love in Alaska...*"

The End

Printed in Great Britain
by Amazon

3d7073cf-a89b-47fa-a758-46c71ef89858R01